Romancing the Lakes of Minnesota
~Spring~

Angeline Fortin
Peg Pierson
Dylann Crush
Kristy Johnson
Katie Curtis
Rose Marie Meuwissen
Ingrid Anderson Sampo
Diane Wiggert
Lanna Farrell
Ann Nardone

A Three Night Stand~ Copyright © 2016 by Angeline Fortin
A Unicorn's Tale ~ Copyright © 2016 by Peg Pierson
Birds of a Feather ~ Copyright © 2016 by Dylann Crush
Fishing for Love ~ Copyright © 2016 by Kristy Johnson
In the Moonlight ~ Copyright © 2016 by Katie Curtis
Nor-Way to Love ~ Copyright © 2016 by Rose Marie Meuwissen
Romance in Time and Space ~ Copyright © 2016 by Ingrid Anderson Sampo
Spring Thaw ~ Copyright © 2016 by Diane Wiggert
Take Your Shirt Off & Stay Forever ~ Copyright © 2016 by Lanna Farrell
The Barn Find ~ Copyright © 2016 by Ann Nardone
All rights reserved.

Names, characters, and incidents depicted in this book are products of the author's imagination or are used fictitiously. Any resemblance to actual events, locales, organizations, or persons, living or dead, is entirely coincidental and beyond the intent of the author or the publisher. No part of this book may be reproduced or transmitted in any form or by any means, electronic or mechanical, including photocopying, recording, or by any information storage and retrieval system, without permission in writing from the publisher.

Published by

Nordic Publishing, LLC.
P. O. Box 923, Prior Lake, MN. 55372
www.NordicPublishing.biz

ISBN: 1530948398
ISBN-13: 978-1530948390

ACKNOWLEDGEMENTS

We would like to offer a special thanks to published authors for Beta Reads and the Minnesota Lakes Anthology Committee. Also for the services provided in publishing this anthology, we would like to thank our cover artist Christopher Edmund, our editor, Lea Burn and Paula Miller for formatting this book.

ROMANCING THE LAKES OF MINNESOTA
~SPRING~

1. **A Three Night Stand** by *Angeline Fortin*
Lake Minnewawa
A one-night stand might be called a mistake but having three one-night stands with the same man only spelled trouble for Zora, especially when he insists on following her home to meet the family. But a day among them shows her there might be more to Ty than meets the eye.

2. **A Unicorn's Tale** by *Peg Pierson*
Schwanz Lake
After years of being bullied, Janelle can't wait to escape her high school nemesis, Hannah, and head off to college. But like a springtime storm, Hannah strikes again, this time wreaking havoc on Janelle's beloved unicorn sculpture just before the county fair competition. Can the magic of a mythological creature mend a fractured friendship and lead to Janelle's happily ever after?

3. **Birds of a Feather** by *Dylann Crush*
Swan Lake
The last thing wedding photographer Wren Arne wants to do is spend a weekend in a canoe, watching warblers with her widowed father. When her ex shows up to play tour guide, she's ready to ditch her binoculars and toss him overboard. But if she can leave her anger in the past and let him back into her heart, their love might be strong enough to spread its wings and fly.

4. **Fishing for Love** by *Kristy Johnson*
   Lake Windigo and Cass Lake
   Upon her father's death, Traci Starr's boyfriend turns abusive, escape seemed like the only option. Retreating to the family cabin on Star Island in Cass Lake, Minnesota, Traci opens herself up to love and the mystical world of Lake Windigo.

5. **In the Moonlight** by *Katie Curtis*
   Lake Sagatagan
   Luke and Anna have a shared dark secret they'll carry to their graves. They've kept tabs on each other all these years, not only because of what they know, but because of what they are.

6. **Nor-Way to Love** by *Rose Marie Meuwissen*
   Lake Harriet
   After her grandfather, Ole Thorson's death, Sonja embraces her Norwegian heritage, its traditions, and one hot photographer from Viking Magazine. Would her inheritance include a Nordic boyfriend?

7. **Romance in Time and Space** by *Ingrid Anderson Sampo*
   Lake Minnetonka
   A grand love for a dead poet draws a college English professor into a romantic time warp with its unique road blocks on the journey to true love.

8. **Spring Thaw** by *Diane Wiggert*
   Lower Hay Lake
   Joy and Paul Givens' marriage has hit an icy patch. Will this pivotal week at the family cabin be enough time to thaw the chill and start them on the path to reconciliation? Or will it send their marriage skidding off the road?

9. **Take Your Shirt Off & Stay Forever** by *Lanna Farrell*
Shirt Lake

After romance author, Reagan Tierney, crashed her car into a snow-filled ditch, she finds herself stuck in the middle of nowhere. Alone, frightened, no cellphone coverage and convinced she's going to freeze to death, she starts to pray. When Officer O'Riley comes to her rescue, he's more than she'd ever hoped for and possibly the hero for her very own happily ever after story.

10. **The Barn Find** by *Ann Nardone*
Bowstring Lake

A classic car, a tragic story, a new beginning and maybe love. Lia learns that you never know what you'll find in a barn.

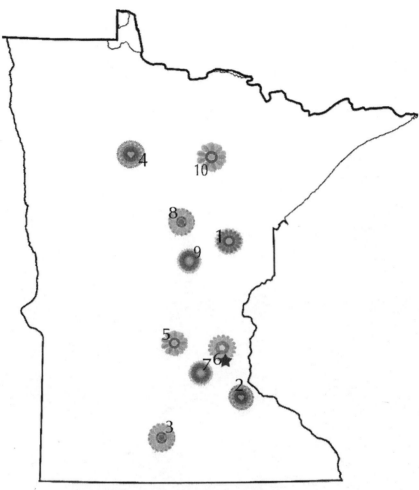

1 Lake Minnewawa, McGregor
2 Schwanz Lake, Rosemount
3 Swan Lake, Nicollet County
4 Lake Windigo & Cass Lake, Cass Lake
5 Lake Sagatagan, Collegeville
6 Lake Harriet, Minneapolis
7 Lake Minnetonka, Wayzata
8 Lower Hay Lake, Pequot Lakes
9 Shirt Lake, Deerwood
10 Bowstring Lake, Deer River

A THREE NIGHT STAND
Angeline Fortin

Lake Minnewawa - McGregor, MN

Squeezing her eyes shut against the bright morning sun, Zora snuggled into the warmth curled around her. She was too comfortable to even think about getting up. Besides, it was Saturday. Life could wait.

A heavy weight fell across her hip, pulling her further into the snug embrace. A deep rumble of contentment sent a quiver through her body. Sensual visions of the previous night flitted through her mind. Tangled limbs. Heaving chests. Hard muscles.

Her sleepy brain kicked into gear and her eyes popped open.

Oh, shit.

Then...

Not again.

She rolled cautiously onto her back, blinking twice at the man lying next to her. Once in disbelief. Once more as an acknowledgement of his stunning beauty. Lashes dark against tanned cheeks. Squared jaw covered in several days' growth of blondish-brown whiskers. Lips softened in repose, but still sensual. So kissable. So tempting.

But her opinion on the matter hadn't changed.

Shit.

After slithering from under his arm, she stealthily dropped to her knees next to the bed and gathered up her clothes, all the while cursing her utter stupidity under her breath.

How could she possibly be so foolish?

Again.

Purse, skirt, shirt...panties. Bra? Oh, there it was. Zora scrambled around on all fours until she had her far-flung belongings bundled in her arms. She hooked her fingers through the straps of her sandals, then stood and padded swiftly on the balls of her feet across the hardwood floor toward the door.

Just as she was about to slip unnoticed from the room, music resounded like the blast of a bullhorn in the silence. Clutching her purse tightly against her chest to muffle the ring of her phone, Zora bounded through the door with all the grace of a hunted gazelle.

Heart stuttering from the expectation of pursuit, she put as much distance between herself and the bedroom as she could. Dropping everything onto the couch, she pulled out her phone and swiped the green button. Not because it was the quickest way to shut the damn thing up, but because she knew the person on the other end would persist in calling until she answered. Even the buzz of the phone on vibrate might wake the beast.

"Mom?"

She could barely hear her mother's voice over the blood rushing through her veins with a dull roar.

"Zora! Good morning," her mother sang across the line. "How are you doing?"

"Fine," she whispered hoarsely, shooting a glance at the open bedroom door.

"You don't sound fine. What's wrong with your voice? Are you getting sick?"

Rolling her eyes, Zora tucked the phone under her chin and started yanking on her clothes. She needed to get out of there...fast. "I'm fine, Mom. Listen, can I call you back in two minutes?"

"What's the matter?"

A low groan, that had nothing to do with her struggle to put on her bra while holding a phone at the same time, escaped her. "Nothing. Seriously, two minutes. Let me call you back."

"Honey, what's wrong?"

"Zora?"

Her name, spoken in a deep, husky timbre, came not from the phone but from the other room and Zora's heart sank.

"Who was that?" her mother asked.

Could this morning get any worse? "No one."

"Zora?"

"No one?" Her mother clucked her tongue. "'No one' isn't calling your name in a voice like that at seven a.m., honey. Who do you have there? Are you practicing safe sex?"

"Oh, God," Zora moaned, shoving her arms into her shirt so hastily the seams popped at the shoulder. "Not now, Mom."

"Can we meet him?"

"No."

"Hey, there."

Mid-tug, she froze at the drowsy male voice. She turned back to the bedroom door and stared at the man who stood there in all his buck-naked glory, running his fingers through his tousled golden hair with a yawn. He could've been immortalized in bronze at that moment and his statue would still draw millions of fans. She couldn't help but sigh.

"Good morning."

"He sounds lovely," her mom breathed into the phone. "I didn't know you were dating anyone. Who is he?"

"Who are you talking to?"

She couldn't have two conversations at one time. Especially when she didn't want to have either of them. "Mom, I'll call you back."

"No need, honey. I can tell you're busy." There was a smirk in her tone. "I just wanted to see what time you're planning on getting here."

"About noon," Zora answered, refusing to meet the curious green eyes boring into her from across the room.

Laughter tinkled from the phone so loud, she knew he could hear it, too. "No need to rush, Zora. We can wait an hour or so longer."

Now she did meet that intriguing gaze, watching one golden brow rise. "No, I'll be on my way in five minutes."

"Now that's a shame," her mom chided. "Why don't you bring him along?"

"No."
"We'd love to meet him."
"God, no."

* * *

With a touch to the screen, Zora hung up on her mother and then tossed the phone onto the couch. Watching Ty watch her, she pulled on the rest of her clothes. His eyes were like pale peridot. Their color had intrigued her right from the start. Hell, everything about him had intrigued her right from the beginning. Still did.

That didn't mean she planned to do anything about it beyond getting out of his apartment as quickly as possible.

"Zora…"

Her phone rang again, blaring Bruno Mars to break the oppressive silence. Snatching it up, she answered without tearing her eyes away from the golden god before her.

"You shouldn't hang up on your mother."

"I'm sorry, Mom."

"Bring him."

"No."

"Do. I want to meet the man who managed a sleepover with you. What's it been? Two years sinc—"

"Mom!"

"See you soon then. Bring him, please."

"No."

A long-suffering sigh. "I love you, honey."

"Love you, too."

Zora's gaze slid to the side as she spoke those last three words. She couldn't look at Ty while she was saying that. It would be too weird. She hung up and slid the phone into her purse then hefted the bag over her shoulder as she stepped into her sandals, tugging the strap up over her heel.

Silence, once again, hung heavily in the room as he waited. She glanced up at him again, suppressing the quiver of renewed desire that washed over her as he drew closer Comfortable in his nudity.

Why not? He was gorgeous.

He stopped just a foot away. His eyes wary, watchful. "You were just going to leave without saying goodbye?"

She shrugged.

"Again?"

Yes, again. And that was the whole problem. This wasn't just a one-night-stand she'd tried to sneak away from. It was her third one-night-stand this month. It might have been slutty if all three hadn't been with the same man.

Ty freakin' MacMillan.

Each time, she'd promised herself it wouldn't happen again. But it did. Again.

And again.

Zora scanned the room, reminding herself of all the reasons she was running away from him. The view of the Mississippi River and the city beyond framed by the floor to ceiling windows. The priceless works of art hanging on the loft's walls. The expensive tech scattered throughout the space.

All the gilded proof they were worlds apart.

"Sorry, I didn't want to wake you. I've got to go." She managed a step back and hiked her purse higher over her shoulder.

Ty caught her hand. "Zora, come on. Stay. Let me take you out to breakfast."

Zora laughed at that. Who went out to breakfast? And she knew he wasn't talking about IHOP. "No, I have a thing today I've got to get to."

"At noon."

She shot him a confused stare.

"I heard you say at noon."

"It's a few hours' drive away," she clarified. "And I still have to stop by my house to pick up some stuff before I go."

"Before we go," he said softly.

Zora's eyes widened. "What? No."

"I heard the invitation all the way across the room." He jerked a thumb toward his previous position by the bedroom door. "I'm coming with you."

"No, you're not."

"I am."

"You. Are. Not."

"Oh, yes, I am."

Gritting her teeth at his firm insistence, Zora turned on her heel and stalked to the condo door. With a crank of the deadbolt and a turn of the handle, she was out in the hall before Ty could cross the room and catch her. Stubborn or not—sculpted muscles or not—Ty wasn't going to come along without any clothes on.

But he did. Rendered speechless by his brazen display, Zora gawked at him before narrowing her eyes. He saw the challenge; his jaw set more stubbornly than her own.

"Don't think I won't do it, Zora. And who do you think would be more embarrassed by me chasing you down the hall with my junk swinging for all the world to see?"

* * *

She'd been stewing silently for the past two hours and twenty-three minutes, Ty noted, checking his watch. Her knuckles were white where she gripped the steering wheel while her cheeks flushed with silent fury. That rage hadn't softened a bit since she'd left his downtown Minneapolis condo, barely giving him time to throw on jeans and a t-shirt, much less shower and shave. He'd chased after her, pulling on his shoes and a striped cardigan in the elevator.

In fact, her anger had gone up a notch when she'd stopped in front of a tidy, but tiny, house on a crowded street east of Lake Nokomis in the southeast corner of town. With a terse command for him to stay in the car, she'd disappeared inside. He'd waited for her, truly uncertain whether she'd intended to abandon him there and sneak out the back. He'd taken the time to study her house, from the precise rows of daffodils lining the walk to the colorfully painted peace symbol hanging on the front door, trying in vain to learn something more about Zora. Something more than the minuscule details she'd chosen to share with him over their three meetings.

To his relief, she'd returned moments later. She'd changed her clothes and was carrying an awkward tower of plastic containers with a brightly wrapped package perched on top. He'd moved to get out and help her put them in the back of her battered hatchback but retreated quickly at her cold glare.

Ty stared out the window as they drove north out of the Cities, hardly even sneaking a peek at her. He didn't need to see her to know she was still wearing that scowl. Obviously, she didn't want him along. Or anywhere near her for that matter. She resented his presence.

He could handle that. What he couldn't deal with was letting her get away from him again.

Twice before, she'd slipped away from him in the early hours of the morning without a word.

And she'd been about to walk away from him without a backward glance. Again.

Why? Something as powerful as the pull between them deserved to be explored not ignored. "Zora..."

With a yank on the steering wheel that jerked the car off the highway and slammed him into the door, Zora pulled into a long driveway. Breaking through the tree line, a rambling cabin with an A-frame in the center caught his attention. Behind it, sunlight bounced of the rippling water of the lake like fireworks. In contrast to the peaceful view, a dozen cars sat parked unceremoniously on the graveled drive and the grass. Bikes of all sizes littered the lawn. Off to the side, a trio of canoes lay stacked like tumbled dominos. Nearby, a rusted aluminum fishing boat with a trolling motor and an old Evinrude outboard on the back rested on a trailer. A faded plastic paddleboat was being tugged toward the water by a platoon of children.

"Nice place," he said at last.

Zora stared at the house for a long moment before shifting her gaze to his.

For a split second his heart stopped before resuming at an accelerated pace. Every time she looked at him, it was the same. Adrenaline, joy, panic, and something else. It had scared the hell out of him the first time he'd seen her. The second time they'd met, the rush had been followed by something more profound. Like a junkie, he wanted to experience the high of being with her continuously.

But she didn't want it. He couldn't figure out why.

This time he wasn't letting her run away until he found out.

"You sure you want to do this?"

Was that a challenge in her voice? Or a forewarning?

"Absolutely."

Her lips lifted in a smirk before she resumed her glower. "Just remember...you asked for it."

She pushed her door open and Ty followed. Unnerved by her knowing smirk, he lingered close by as she went to the rear of the car and lifted the hatch. This time, she didn't hesitate to load him up with the stack of food containers, keeping the wrapped present for herself to carry.

Before they could make more than a step in the direction of the house, the front door opened. An older woman darted down the porch steps with a delighted squeal and an energetic wave of her arms that Ty didn't normally associate with a woman of advancing years.

"There's my baby girl!" she cried.

Or mothers for that matter, he amended inwardly, watching with a twinge of envy as the woman pulled Zora into an embrace, squashing the package between them. She rocked Zora back and forth, laughing merrily, before pulling away and kissing her cheek. Joy and pride radiated from her.

It was...sweet.

Zora's unfettered smile was even sweeter.

"You brought him."

The smile slipped away at the woman's obvious elation. Zora turned to him with an arched brow. "I didn't bring him. I was forced into submission, remember?"

With a polite smile, Ty shifted his load to one arm and held out his hand. "It's a pleasure to meet you, Mrs....?"

* * *

Oh, the poor, innocent man. For a tiny moment, Zora felt sorry for him, knowing what was to come.

Sure enough, her mother waved his hand away and enfolded Ty in her arms, hugging him as if he were one of her own. "Never mind that. I'm Marigold, or call me Mari. I'm sure we'll be the best of friends."

"Thank you, Mari," he said awkwardly, though there was something close to pleasure in his eyes. "I'm Tyler Mac—"

"This is Ty, Mom."

"So happy to meet you, Ty!" Mari kissed his cheek and backed away, beaming at him as if he were some sort of savior. "Zora doesn't date much and it's been a long time since she's brought anyone home to meet the family."

Zora rolled her eyes.

"Thank you for the invitation," Ty said politely. "I'm happy to meet Zora's family."

Mari patted his cheek with a grin. "Aren't you sweet? But we're just getting started. Come inside, let me introduce you around."

Her mother looped her arm through his and steered Ty toward the house. "Tell me, have you two been dating long?"

"Well, I've been trying. If I can convince her—"

"*Convince* her? Oh, everyone's just going to love you!"

He glanced over his shoulder at Zora with something akin to panic as her mom tugged him up the porch steps. On some level, she felt a stab of pity for him. For what was about to happen. Who he was, how he was raised, couldn't prepare him for what was about to befall him. She might've found a moment in the last couple of hours to provide some warning. Prep him for what awaited. However, she was still irritated...and he was only getting what he asked for.

"Everyone!" Mari called, tugging Ty behind her. Zora trailed along as they passed through the house and out the back door to the deck spanning the back of the cabin. As much as she dreaded what was about to happen, she knew she had to see it. Like watching a train wreck. "Come and meet Zora's special friend..."

Ah yes, she'd almost forgotten how her mother could put such a singular emphasis on the word.

"...Ty. Let's make him feel welcome."

They did. *En masse*. Even from Zora's perspective, it was a cringe-worthy sight. Dozens of them surrounded him, each one not hesitating to hug him like a long-lost brother upon introduction.

"This is my daughter Willow, her husband, Ryan, and their kids, Ash, Micha, Mark and Zen." As if her mother expected him to remember all the names. But that was only the beginning. "My daughter Lyric, and her life partner, Cassidy. That's my other daughter, Trinity, with her almost-husband, Keith, and their boys, Free, Justice, Augie, and...oh, where is he? And John," she said, pointing, and Zora could see the horror on Ty's face when the little boy flung his arms around Ty's legs and grinned up at him with a gap-toothed smile.

Still, the ordeal wasn't over. Barely taking a moment to breathe, Mari went on, "My son, Hale, and his wife, Meghan, and baby Dylan. Here's my oldest daughter, Dharma, and her husband, Joe and their six kids..."

Her multitude of siblings, nieces, nephews, aunts, uncles, cousins—all of them were here to celebrate the seventieth birthday of her father, who came last to greet Ty with his usual mellow smile that belied the chaos surrounding them.

Finally the crowd dispersed, leaving Ty shell-shocked as if he were coming upon a pack of crazed hippies dancing naked in a field.

He might as well have. Somehow her entire family had fully absorbed every nuance of her parents' bohemian, peace-loving ways. To the last, they were free spirits. Free with their affection, love, opinions, and bullshit. Even Zora, the youngest of the eight siblings—the surprise of their later years—wasn't much different.

Even so, her upbringing wasn't the least of what cultural differences filled the wide expanse between them.

Still, feeling a spurt of sympathy, she freed an icy beer from a nearby cooler and silently handed it to him. He twisted off the top and tilting his head back, taking a long swig.

God, was she actually thinking that even his stubbled neck was sexy? Zora glanced away as he drank half the bottle.

"Well? Are you having fun yet?"

"Your family is...exuberant."

"Yup, they're a gift that just keeps on giving."

The corner of his mouth quirked but the smile slipped away a moment later. He drank again, staring out over the lake, or maybe he was contemplating the dozens of family members peppering the lawn.

"I don't think I've ever been hugged that much in my entire life."

The words were so soft, Zora wasn't sure if he was speaking to her or just to himself, but something inside her chest shifted at the notion he might not be joking...or exaggerating.

"Aunt Zora!" Her six-year-old niece, Harmony, latched onto her hand, drawing her attention away from the unwelcome compassion for the man beside her. "Are you going to come in the paddle boat with me?"

"Of course, baby girl! We ladies have to stick together, right?" Gripping her hand gratefully, Zora grinned at Ty. "Harmony's outnumbered by all her boy cousins so...sorry."

"But..."

"Sorry, Ty, the boat only holds two people. Oh, here comes Uncle Hi to keep you company. Have fun!"

* * *

She'd waved him off and abandoned him without a backward glance. Ty supposed she thought he deserved whatever might happen after he'd forced his company on her all day. Perhaps he did.

Between conversations with curious aunts, grumbling uncles,

inquiring cousins, and blatantly nosy siblings, he'd caught sight of her here and there. A glimpse of her smile, the sound of her laughter—punctuated by the occasional snort—had him taking all the interrogations without offense.

God, it did something to him to see her so happy. To see her playing with her niece and nephews with childlike glee. To see the April sun shining off her lovely face, to watch her blond hair swaying in the breeze, to see her blue eyes dancing with joy. He wished *he* could make her that happy. In fact, he knew he could if she'd give him half a chance.

As the afternoon began to wane, Ty managed to catch her alone in the kitchen as she refilled a jug of lemonade.

"Let me carry that for you."

"It's okay. I've got it."

"Zora..."

"I said, I got it." She cast him a patently false, tight smile and picked up the jug before turning away...again. He had to give it to her, she was consistent.

He took the jug and set it back on the table. Catching her by the hand so she couldn't run away, he stepped closer. Her gaze darted from left to right, searching for an escape, but he held her chin, forcing her to meet his eyes.

"Come on, Zora," he whispered. "Give me something."

"Hey, I didn't invite you, Ty, my mom did."

"A minute. That's all." Ty sighed. Yes, she was consistent and stubborn. "A smile?" He stroked his thumb down her cheek, reveling in the way she unconsciously leaned into him. "Have some mercy on me? I spent over a half an hour listening to your Uncle Hi lobby for the legalization of marijuana."

"Really? I'm surprised he even realizes it's illegal. Certainly hasn't stopped him."

Her eyes flashed with laughter, the same expression that sparked his interest when they'd met weeks before. That dry humor, touched with sarcasm. She'd made him laugh as he hadn't in years. They'd talked and talked for hours until he'd given in to temptation and kissed her. They hadn't really talked since.

He knew her body intimately, but what he wanted was to know more about her. However, she was already sidling away.

"Stay with me, Zora. Talk to me."

"Ty…"

"What? What is it?"

* * *

He was close enough she could feel the heat radiating off him. His fingertips traced a line along her jaw before teasing her earlobe and sliding into her hair. Panicked desire shook her as his lips grazed her cheek, but she couldn't run. He'd had her at his mercy since the moment she'd first clapped eyes on him.

Her lashes fluttered closed and she helplessly tilted her face up to his at the first touch of his mouth against hers. Their mouths melded. His tongue traced the seam of her lips, coaxing her to part them. Powerless to stop, she surrendered to the desire quivering through her and let him in. He advanced but didn't attack, instead teasing and testing.

"*Ah*, Zora," he groaned against her mouth. "Why are you fighting this? It's more than just being mad at me for coming along today. I know that. But what is it? You won't give me your number, or even your full name for that matter. You sleep with me…"

Zora flushed bright red at the reminder and tried to pull away, but he held her captive with nothing more than a finger beneath her chin.

"…then you sneak out before I wake up. I don't know where to find you or how to get in touch with you."

Yet, somehow, they'd kept bumping into each other. She'd been attracted to Ty from the moment she'd met him. That first night, he'd just been Ty, a guy full of charm and sexy dance moves that had seduced her into her first one-night-stand ever. Waking up in his condo, she'd been appalled by her behavior but even more so by the discovery of who he really was.

The next time their paths crossed, she'd been determined to keep him at arm's length. Even though she'd attempted to turn a deaf ear to his persistent conversation, she'd first found herself reluctantly smiling at his stories, then laughing helplessly. Soon, she'd been spilling her life story as if in a confessional. After baring her soul, she'd bared her body once more to his irresistible passion.

And bolted again, like a sinner trying to escape the relentless pull of a hell.

It'd taken longer that third time for him to find her. She'd avoided all her normal hangouts, knowing she wouldn't be able to resist him again. And she hadn't. He was like no one she'd ever known. He wasn't only handsome, but smart and funny. Not only interesting, but *interested*. In her. He had a way of making her feel like she was the center of his world.

Falling into his arms and his bed was the easy part though. Falling for the rest of him...well, she was on the cusp of the greatest leap of all.

"Ty..."

"What?" he whispered huskily, sending another shudder of desire through her. "What is it? What's making you run from this? From me?"

She could have given him some old line about how it wasn't him. It was her. But honestly, it *was* him. Everything about him, as tempting as it was, screamed at her to run away.

"Zora? Look at me."

She did, as if he held her in his thrall. Perhaps he did. She'd never been so powerless, so unable to follow her own good common sense. Looking at him wasn't helping either. His rugged masculinity had mesmerized her that first night. Sculpted male perfection, his jaw covered in a few days' growth of dark blond whiskers that softened his hard angles. Every last feature was flawless, but it was his eyes that always got her. Under thick brown brows, they pierced her to the core.

Every. Damn. Time.

To say nothing about the rest of him. Well over six feet of long limbs, thick muscles that only a personal trainer and a lot of spare time could produce, every rise and ripple of his chest and abs begged to be adored. And she had…in every possible way. Repeatedly.

And then run from him, just as he said.

All because of whom he was.

Stepping out of his reach, Zora snatched up the jug of lemonade, holding it like a shield between them. "I've got stuff to do."

"Come on, Zora! Haven't you gotten the payback you wanted?" he said with frustration, scrunching his fingers into his hair until it stood straight up. "I've spent the last three hours talking to everyone here but you. I've been grilled on my politics, religious views, and dating history. Your mother probably knows more about my love life than you do. A shrink couldn't have wrung anything more out of me. Don't think I don't know you consider all of this my punishment for forcing you to bring me along."

A twinge of something squeezed her heart. Yes, it was a pretty harsh sentence for the unsuspecting.

"Ty…"

No, she steeled herself. Not just Ty. Tyler Lawrence MacMillan the Third. His family owned one of the largest farm equipment conglomerates in the country. Hell, in the world. They were worth billions. He was.

She hadn't known it when she met him. If she had, she would have run the other way immediately. She knew it was contrary to what most women would do when meeting a handsome billionaire, but Zora had her reasons. After a failed relationship with another one-percent snob, she wasn't prepared to even attempt a second.

What he was would never mesh with all of this. Surely, he could see that now?

"Go back to your people, Ty. You don't belong here."

"My people? What is that supposed to mean?"

"Exactly what it sounds like." She put the lemonade back down but it hit the table harder than she'd intended. The resounding thud fueled the irritation that had been simmering all day. "No one asked you to come along. Yes, I know what my mom said but you weren't actually invited. Not by me. You just made your own rules and did what you wanted. I'm sure it comes naturally. Well, you might be able to push and shove your way around the world, but if you don't like what comes back at you, that isn't my fault. You got yourself into this."

"Hey, did I say I wasn't having a good time?"

"Ha! Like *you* would have a good time here." She swept her arm toward the window as if it framed all that was wild, dysfunctional, and terrifying about her family. Blood surged through her veins; she'd known it would come to this. "Just go back where you belong."

"I think you're getting all riled up over nothing, Zora."

"I don't get riled up," she shot back. "I never get riled up. My parents are pacifists. They were at Woodstock, for Pete's sake. Dharma was probably conceived in the middle of a cornfield. Or right in front of a crowd of millions. They preach peace and love and tolerance and mean every word of it. I've never raised my voice in my life."

"Yet you're doing a fine imitation of it now."

She opened and closed her mouth like a fish then ground her teeth and turned on her heel, slamming the kitchen door as she left.

* * *

With a sigh, Ty picked up the lemonade and took it outside. After finding its spot on the table of food and drinks, he searched for the cooler and another beer.

"Give me one of those, will you?"

Ty glanced up from his dig through the ice to see Zora's father standing nearby. Pulling a bottle out of the cooler, he held it out but Walter, if he remembered the name right—it was difficult to think it was the correct one, given it's normalcy in a sea of hippie names—shook his head.

"None of that IPA nonsense for me. Give me one of those Schell's there."

With a nod, Ty swapped the beers, grabbed one of the same for himself, and stood. In unison, they twisted off the caps and took a long swallow. Walter gave the bottle a nod of appreciation.

"You know they've been brewing this down there in New Ulm since about 1860?"

"Yes, sir, I knew that."

"Humph." Walter nodded again. "You know, I like you, son. You took to this mob we've got here real well."

"I've enjoyed the day, sir."

That earned him a chuckle. "Day's only beginning. Nope, I do like you, but I'm afraid you might not stand half a chance with my daughter."

Something deep inside of Ty froze at the certainty in the man's voice. "Why is that?"

"I know who you are." Walter took another long drink of his beer, long enough to make Ty think the kindly old man was toying with him. "Willow recognized you. Her husband is a lawyer down in the Cities. Said she met you at some fundraiser last winter. You own MacMillan, Inc."

"Only one-seventh of it."

Walter harrumphed again. "Enough of it to put you out of favor with Zora. Frankly, I was surprised she even brought you along…once I knew who you were. Still, she's sleeping with you. I suppose that counts for something."

Ty flinched at the matter-of-fact reference to what he'd assumed was a very private physical relationship.

"You two being safe?"

He cringed again. His own parents would never dream of asking such a thing. "Your wife already broached this subject."

Walter nodded again. "Well, if she's satisfied."

He didn't even want to *think* about who the old man was referring to with that vague statement. Instead, he got back to the problem at hand. "Why would who I am make a difference to Zora? Most women would love to date a bill—"

"I'm going to stop you right there, son. One thing you've got to know about the Rosenberg women, they aren't like most women."

Rosenberg? Well, at least he finally had a last name.

Walter continued. "Zora's been pampered her whole life being the baby of the family. The last of the bunch. Frankly, she was a damned surprise, but a happy one. Ain't nothing your money can buy her she doesn't already have."

Unwillingly, Ty pictured her battered hatchback, her tiny house, but it was as if the old man could read his thoughts.

"I'm talking about the other stuff, son. She's got love, our love. Happiness in her work. Joy in her life. But someone else…suppose some might say someone else like you, came along and made her question that. Then doubt it. Then made her feel all the worse by holding who she wasn't against her. Said she'd never belong in his world, never fit in with his people."

His people, just like she'd said. At least he knew now what she'd meant. Whoever told her that was a bastard. And an idiot. Zora could win the heart of even the coldest society bitches out there. Maybe even his mother's.

"So, she's punishing me because of how someone else treated her?" he asked, dread sneaking into his heart.

Again, Walter shook his head. "She's not punishing you. It's not about anger, or even forgiveness."

"It's fear," Ty said, the same moment he realized it.

Walter nodded and tipped up his beer again. "I do like you, son. Zora…well, I'm pretty sure she does, too."

"Why's that?"

"She wouldn't have brought you here if she didn't…no matter how you tried to force her hand."

* * *

"He's cute, Zora," Dharma said over the rim of her wine glass. "If I weren't so in love with Joe, I might fight you for him. Remind me, I am in love with Joe, right?"

Willow laughed and rose from her chair to drop another log

onto the flames raging in the huge fire pit set between the house and the lake. The early April afternoon cooled off as the sun sank in the sky and the breeze off Lake Minnewawa started picking up. "You are. Desperately. Now, me? I might be okay with having a few issues with Ryan if it meant snagging me a billionaire. Well done, Zora."

Just as they had when they'd first heard the news of Ty's identity, all her sisters sighed and craned their necks to give him another appreciative once over. Even Zora couldn't help herself. Under the auspice of stretching her neck, she peered over her shoulder to where Ty was laughing over a game of horseshoes with her brother and many brothers-in-law. They all liked him. Even her usually discriminative father seemed to like him. As for Ty…

The day hadn't gone at all as she'd imagined. He hadn't run screaming from the property pulling at his hair or thrown himself into the lake. No one would have blamed him. Her enormous, boisterous family was a lot to take on a whole. Even the one other time she'd dared to introduce a man to her family—in small stages, to ease him in—it had been too much.

She'd never tried it again. She loved her family and when she made a commitment someday, she wouldn't stand for anything less than the same level of devotion all her in-laws had given. That was part of the reason she'd been so determined to avoid Ty. Becoming attached to someone who was certain to let her down had been inadvisable.

But would he? Over the past month, he'd proven himself to be persistent, a quality as attractive as his looks and wit.

As for her, she would have body-blocked any of the women in her family or otherwise to be the first one to his side. Her determination to keep him at arm's length was faltering. It had been all afternoon. Look what a pile of mush she'd become after just one kiss!

But far from the retribution Ty was right in believing she'd meant to deal him, he'd seemed to actually enjoy her chaotic family, and appeared truly interested in what she knew were the often disjointed ramblings of her great-aunt, laughed at her cousin's horrible jokes, helped with kitchen duty, and played football with her slew of nephews.

She'd learned more about him by watching his interactions with her family than in the hours of conversation they'd shared over the past month. If anything, the day had only shown her more about Tyler MacMillan to admire. More to love.

Zora bit her tongue and swallowed a large gulp of her wine. Could it be possible? Could she...?

"Just go for it, honey." Her mom eased down beside her and patted her hand. "Hasn't he taken enough of a beating today to prove to you he isn't your typical, imperious rich boy?"

Still Zora wavered indecisively. "Oh, Momma! What if I...?" The thought trailed off into nothingness. There were so many *ifs* she didn't even know how to express them.

"Sure, baby, I understand," her mom replied calmly. "But what if you don't?"

* * *

"Hey."

Ty felt a jolt of surprise and pleasure in equal parts as Zora's sweet voice filled his ears. Turning, he took in her red cheeks, mussed hair, and oversized sweatshirt in a sweeping glance of appreciation. His gaze settled on her full lower lip as she gnawed on it in a manner that had been driving him mad for a month.

"Having fun yet?" The question was the same one she'd asked hours ago, though this time it lacked in the dry sarcasm.

"I am," he said sincerely. The men around them drifted away, leaving them relatively alone, the glow of the fire pit between them and her family. "It's been a pleasant adventure."

"That might be the kindest thing anyone's ever said about us."

"It's the truth." He set aside his drink. "Are you ready to head back to the Cities?"

Zora quirked an amused brow. "No, we're spending the night. Hey, you didn't ask the duration of the visit when you decided to come along."

"And you chose not to tell me?" he asked. "More of your punishment?"

"Haven't you had enough?" She didn't let him answer. "I've been drinking and so have you. A few hours of driving is a few too many."

Ty gazed at the log cabin and then back at the crowd still gathered around the fire. It didn't take a great mathematician to do the calculations. "So you have a bedroom here?"

"I do." He sagged in relief, but she continued. "But at gatherings like this, I give up my bed to one of my married siblings and sack out in the living room with the rest of the unmarried kids."

"You mean the actual kids?" He cringed at the thought. There must have been thirty of them. Not one of them past the tween years.

"You're welcome to a couch," she offered. "If you think you can handle it."

"Is that a challenge?"

"Maybe." Zora shrugged. "I doubt you've ever had to sleep on a couch in your life. Beyond your own," she added when he started to argue. "Listen, I get it's not what you're used to. I tried to warn you. I tried to—"

"Avoid this entirely," he finished for her. "I've learned a few things from your family today, Zora."

It was her turn to grimace. "They have no filters. They shouldn't have told you anything."

"You should have," Ty said softly. "Or better yet, you should have had some faith in me. Some faith in us."

"Faith?" she laughed. "I knew what would happen."

"And yet, you didn't, did you?" he pushed. Taking her hand, he covered it with both of his. "I'm still here, aren't I? I'm not like that other guy, Zora. I would never think less of you for any reason. You're intelligent and challenging. I want more of that. You make me think and laugh. Your family makes me laugh like my own hasn't in years. In fact, I can only hope you don't run screaming from *my* family. They can be a bunch of asses."

"Because I'm not good enough for them?"

"No, because they'll know in a heartbeat how much better you are."

* * *

Surprised by the veiled compliment, Zora caught her lip between her teeth again, worrying it, as she turned away and gazed out over the lake now reflecting the light of the rising moon.

Ty's warmth pressed against her back as he wrapped his arms around her shoulders and pulled her tightly against him. He felt so good, so right, just as he had that morning and the other two mornings she'd awoken with next to him.

"I want more of this, Zora. More of us. Please don't run from me any more."

"It's just sex, Ty. Good sex, but that's it." It was a lie but he seemed to know her well enough already to sense her impulse to bolt from the unknown.

"That's not it, Zora. This is more than that. It's not the sex."

She tilted her head back and raised a brow.

He had the good grace to flush. "I'm not saying it isn't good. It's incredible." He fell silent for a moment before turning her to face him. His pale eyes glittered in the firelight as he brushed a strand of hair back from her temple. "To be honest, it's even more than that. You bring me to my knees, Zora. I've never…" Ty ran a hand through his hair, making it stand on end. He did that a lot when he was tense or thoughtful. The habit was oddly endearing. "It's never been like that before. Not for me." His gaze slid away, his expression pained. She'd never imagined hearing such heartfelt words from him. "You break me, Zora. It's like you rip out a piece of me and take it with you each time. I know we haven't known each other very long, but I'm yours."

God, he'd broken her as well. A tear escaped the corner of her eye and splashed onto her cheek, her heart torn from her own chest by the emotion of his confession.

"That is, if you…and that whole crazy bunch over there watching us…will have me."

Choked by tears, she could only stare at him. She didn't need to look behind her. She knew they were all watching and would always be watching out for her.

"Will you say something?"

"Ty…"

Zora ran her fingers over his whiskered cheek and pulled him to her with a sob that instantly flared to passion when they kissed. Ty lifted her tightly against him until her toes barely touched the ground. Still he didn't release her, deepening the kiss as the whole Rosenberg clan cheered and whistled.

Knowing they were being watched should have cooled their passion but they clung to one another.

Zora smiled up at him. "There's my dad's camper shell in the garage if you want a bed tonight."

"To share?" he whispered, shifting his gaze from her to her family and back again. "Won't they care?"

"Not as long as…"

"We have safe sex," they finished together and laughed once more before disappearing hand-in-hand into the shadows.

ABOUT THE AUTHOR

Angeline Fortin is the author of historical and time-travel romance offering her readers fun, sexy and often touching tales of romance.

Her most recent release, *Taken: A Laird for All Time Novel*, was recently awarded the Virginia Romance Writers 2015 Holt Medallion Award for Paranormal Romance.

With a degree in US History from UNLV and having previously worked as a historical interpreter at Colonial Williamsburg, Angeline brings her love of history and Great Britain to the forefront in settings such as Victorian London and Scotland.

As a former military wife, Angeline has lived from the west coast to the east, from the north to the south and uses those experiences along with her favorite places to tie into her time travel novels as well.

Angeline is a native Minnesotan who recently relocated back to the land of her birth. She is a PAN member of the Romance Writers of America and Midwest Fiction Writers. She lives in Apple Valley outside the Twin Cities with her husband, two children and three dogs.

You can follow Angeline on:
Facebook — http://on.fb.me/1fBD1qq
Twitter — https://twitter.com/AngelineFortin
Google+ — http://bit.ly/1hWXSGB
Tumblr — https://www.tumblr.com/blog/angeline-fortin
Pinterest — https://www.pinterest.com/angelinefortin1/

You can also visit her website at www.angelinefortin.com or just send her a message at fortin.angeline@gmail.com.

Enjoy!
Peg

A UNICORN'S TALE
Peg Pierson

Schwanz Lake - Rosemount, MN

A cool spring breeze floated through the window of the visual arts room.

Janelle took a step back from her creation and with a twinkle in her eye, said, "Unicorns are so rare that most people believe they are extinct."

The *Dakota County Tribune* reporter grinned. It was a very impressive sculpture. A nine-foot unicorn commissioned by the Rosemount High School independent studies program. The young artist, a spunky blonde senior, was just as impressive. An honor student, a speech team leader, and a scholarship recipient to University of Minnesota, Miss Janelle O'Leary was a delight.

"Thanks for sharing your project with me and all my readers. I'd be honored to come back when your…what is his name? Is all finished."

"William. That's the name of my unicorn. And of course, I'd love to have you come see him when he's done."

The bell rang and Janelle smoothed down a piece of metal siding on the sculpture. She climbed down the ladder and gazed at William. He was coming along even better than she'd expected. He'd lived in her imagination for as long as she could remember. Now, he was coming to life! Well, coming into existence, at least.

"Hey, stop gawking at your masterpiece. We'll be late for gym." Marcia tucked an errant green lock of hair behind her multi-pierced ear and tugged on her best friend's arm.

"He's worth gawking at," Janelle said, setting her hands on her waist. "Imagine what he'd look like as a prince."

Marcia tilted her head. "*Huh?* A prince? He's a unicorn, Janelle. Have you been sniffing the glue you're using on him?"

Janelle chuckled. "No. It's an ancient legend. I've got a book all about it. A virtuous maiden can transform a unicorn into a man, usually a prince or a knight."

"How about a math tutor?" Marcia said, adjusting her backpack. "I'm getting a D in algebra."

"I know it's silly but I've fantasized about William for as long as I can remember."

"Yeah." Marcia cleared her throat. "*Uh*, Janelle? Why William? Shouldn't it have a more horsey kinda name? Like, My Little Pony or Seabiscuit? Flicka?"

Janelle rolled her eyes. "*Duh*. It's not a horse. *He* is a unicorn, and I named him after Prince William."

Marcia smacked her forehead with her hand. "Of course! Well, let's get going, Princess Kate, we commoners must appear in the royal gym class. You need to beat Hannah in badminton." She turned for the door.

"I'm coming, I'm coming, but seriously," Janelle held her arms up like a game show hostess, "he is magnificent. I think he'll take a ribbon at the county fair."

"Yeah yeah, ribbon-schmibbon. Gym. Class. Now."

* * *

Janelle held the ice pack to her eye. "Glad we got to class on time," she said to Marcia. "Today was super fun."

"Hannah is a scuzzy dirt bag." Marcia tugged her anime T-shirt over her head.

"A scuzzy dirt bag with laser-like precision smacking a birdy."

Marcia peeked around the lockers to make sure they were alone. "I don't care if her dad is vice-principal. We have to do something to get back at her. You know she'll only get a pretend punishment."

Janelle snorted. "What did she get last time? Oh, yeah! They made her organize the football banquet…with Luke the Lips Quarterback as her assistant."

"Grueling." Marcia sat down and threw her arm over Janelle's shoulders. "You're super smart. Think. What can we do to Hannah? She's been bullying you since the fifth grade. Nobody does anything."

"My mom tried!" Janelle shot Marcia a scathing glare.

"Hey," Marcia squeezed Janelle's shoulder, "I know. Your mom is great. I know she tried, but she's up against the whole faculty. Nobody is gonna help us. Hannah has impurity."

Janelle smiled at her best friend. "I think she does have that, Marcia, but I believe the word you meant was *immunity*."

"Whatever." Marcia popped up off the bench. "So, what's the plan, oh, wise one?"

Janelle stood up. "Nothing. In a few weeks, we'll graduate and I will never have to deal with Hannah and her bullying again. We're not going to stoop to her level."

Marcia frowned. "Well, crap. Are you sure? I'd really like to see Hannah get what she deserves."

"She will," Janelle said. "Mom always says, what goes around comes around."

"Well, I hope it's a big ole tractor trailer that comes around into Hannah."

Janelle tried hard not to smile. And failed completely. "It's sad, really. She and I were best friends when we were kids. We used to do everything together. She was even crazier about unicorns than I was." Janelle stood up. "We used to read my mythology book over and over, pretending we could conjure up a unicorn in my bedroom."

"Oh, exciting." Marcia rolled her eyes. "Sorry I missed that."

"We were kids!" Janelle started toward the door. "I just don't get her. It's like she just woke up one morning hating me."

* * *

"Oh, I just can't stand that goody-two-shoes bitch." Hannah rolled over and stared at the canopy over her queen-sized bed. "God! She's such a suck up, Ava. I can't believe she'll be class speaker for graduation."

"You so should have gotten that. I thought your speech was awesome."

Hannah snorted. "The committee sure didn't. I'm so sick of her always getting everything she wants. Life is always perfect for Janelle. I wish she could feel what it's like to be second best for once. First in speech, class president—*uh*, it's so frustrating!"

"O.M.G. Hannah, I've got it!" Ava held up her iPad, showing an article from the *Dakota County Tribune* with a picture of Janelle, grinning next to her sculpture.

Hannah's dark brown eyes lit up like coals from hell. "Ava. You are the best friend ever."

* * *

"Your mom should totally be on *The Voice*." Marcia grunted as she helped move William off the trailer and onto the front lawn of Janelle's house.

Janelle chuckled and wiped her brow. "Nah, Mom doesn't like to sing alone. She just likes singing with her group."

Just then, Carol O'Leary burst from the house carrying a dish of pumpkin spice bars and sang out, "Here I come to save the daaaaay! I've got snacks upon my traaaaay!"

Marcia shook her head, sending her now-pink locks swirling around. "And you were saying?"

"Oh, Janelle!" Carol set the goodies on the picnic table and rushed up to see her daughter's sculpture. "He is beautiful!"

And he was. William was cool, metallic silver with large round eyes fashioned from clear-blue crystal pieces alight with warmth and magic. His mane of doll's hair fluttered in the soft spring breeze and his curled front legs looked as though he were about to climb into the clouds.

"I'm glad you like him, Mom. He's staying here with you when I go to college."

Marcia nabbed a gooey pumpkin bar. "Yeah, but first a little side trip to the county fair!"

Carol walked around the statue. "I know I'm your mother, but I do think William here has a great shot at a ribbon."

Janelle tilted her head and took in the sight of her project. "Well, ribbon or not, I love him. Unicorn legends have been around forever. Literally. Some say they are simply good luck, some that their horn can turn poison into safe water. And of course," Janelle stood up on tiptoes and stroked his neck, "with the right spell, a pure maiden can magically turn him into a prince."

Janelle looked around her. Spring had brought blossoms and butterflies to her home. The grass had turned a brilliant green all the way down to the lake behind the house where birds flew above dark cerulean water.

A sense of melancholy hit her in the chest. She was an academic at heart and thrilled to have the chance to study at the university. But leaving home, leaving her wonderful, musical, whimsical mother, would not be easy. She glanced back at William. Majestic and mystical. She'd spent months sketching and planning. Leaving him wouldn't be easy either.

"Hey, daydreamer?" Marcia called over. "Please come eat some of the pumpkin bars before I collapse into a diabetic coma!"

* * *

Hannah finished off her second Red Bull and circled back, driving past Janelle's house again. The fair would start tomorrow.

And it would start and end without William the Unicorn.

It would crush Janelle. She'd worked almost the entire year on the project and waking up tomorrow morning to find it in little metal pieces all over the lawn would destroy her.

Hannah had also been accepted to the University of Minnesota, thanks to her dad's connections. Little Miss Smarty Pants had a scholarship, of course. Hannah sighed.

The unicorn was actually pretty cool. She'd gone to the visual arts room to see it in person and now she almost felt bad.

Almost.

* * *

"Sweetie, I'm going to be late tonight," Carol called out from the kitchen. "Late rehearsal for our performance at the fair. Love you!" The back door clicked shut.

Janelle brushed her teeth and climbed into bed, trying to convince herself that the fair tomorrow didn't matter. But it did.

She'd worked so hard on every detail of William. He was exactly what she had seen in her dreams.

Well, not everything from her dreams.

Her fantasy had been of a beautiful white unicorn galloping through a meadow of wildflowers. Spring sunshine glinting in her hair as she said the magic words to turn William into a handsome prince!

Janelle giggled at her own silly thoughts. "I'm such a dork." She shook her head and punched her pillow.

It was adolescent. And completely ridiculous. But it was a wonderful dream. One that had gotten her through many a miserable night after being tormented at school by Hannah.

At least Hannah would be forever in the past. Graduation was coming up. Then no more Hannah. With that happy thought, Janelle snuggled under her sheets and fell asleep.

But a scant thirty minutes later, she was awakened by a loud bang.

She tossed back her covers and ran barefoot into the kitchen. Peering out the window, she gasped. The soft moonlight illuminated William.

And Hannah.

Janelle rushed to the front door and flew down the steps to where William had been brutally destroyed. He was in two pieces. His head lay on the grass, the rest of him stuck in the front bumper of a black SUV. Hannah, her hands on the twisted metal, glanced up at Janelle with an evil glint in her eyes.

"What are you going to do *huh*, smarty pants? Call the police? Call your mommy?"

The anger hit Janelle like a freight train. All the years of bullying and mistreatment seemed to surge through her veins. "Get the hell away from William, you disgusting pig!"

"Ha!" Hannah tugged at the sculpture, trying to dislodge it from the bumper. "Oh, finally some anger from Miss Perfect!"

Janelle threw herself at her nemesis. "You've gone too far this time, Hannah." Janelle pulled back her fist and decked Hannah right in the mouth.

Hannah reeled back and fell on her butt. Yowling, she pushed to her feet. "You bitch! How dare you hit me!"

"Me? Are you kidding? I should have punched you in the fifth grade when you stole my Christmas painting and threw it in the trash!"

Hannah wiped her bloody lip. "It was a stupid picture. You are such a sappy dork. I mean, really, with Santa hugging your mommy and you sitting on a unicorn? Seriously? Your mom is just as dumb as you."

Janelle saw red. "Oh, you evil, evil witch! You are so mean. I've tried to be nice, I've tried to turn the other cheek, but you just won't give up."

"Well, it's your fault!" Janelle noticed tears sliding down Hannah's cheeks. "If you hadn't invited me to go see *The Nutcracker* that night, my mom would still be here."

Janelle blinked. Then shook her head. "Oh my God! It is so not my fault that your mom ran away with that dancer." She bent over and grasped her knees. "All these years you've been mean to me, and started rumors, because of that?"

Hannah narrowed her eyes. "Yes. If Mom had never met that asshole then she would still be here with my dad and me. You and your stupid ballet ruined my life. And my dad's! And you always get everything. Now you even get to deliver the speech at graduation. Do you have any idea how disappointed my dad is in me? I'm so sick of being compared to you. No matter what I do, I'll never be as smart or talented as you."

Hannah reached down and yanked out one of William's blue crystal eyes.

"Noooo!" Janelle rammed Hannah, knocking her back onto the ground.

Then the fighting really got crazy. The girls battled. They swung, hit, punched, and hissed. They rolled all over the lawn and the unicorn.

They finally finished fighting. Dirty and exhausted, they lay on their backs looking up at the night sky, panting.

Janelle spoke first. "Even though it so is not my fault, I am really sorry about what happened to your mom. And I'm not sorry that I've done well in school and stuff, but I am sorry your dad made you feel bad."

"Well," Hannah gingerly touched a loose tooth, "I guess it isn't your fault. I've just always been so mad." She slowly stood up.

Getting to her feet, Janelle pulled a branch from her hair. "And you kinda can't blame your mom, either. That guy's tights were really tight."

Despite everything, both girls laughed until the image of Janelle's project glared up at them from its fallen perch, like a corpse looming up from the grave.

Janelle collapsed next to him, shoulders shaking with her sobs.

"Oh, Janelle." Hannah sat down next to her. "Oh, my God, I'm so sorry. I know I came here to do this but now…"

Janelle flopped over on William and continued to cry. She'd worked so hard, and she loved him so much. The fair tomorrow was the least of it. She felt like a part of her lay on the ground, brutalized and banged up beyond recognition. This was the worst thing Hannah had ever done.

And that was saying a lot.

Consumed by her grief, Janelle didn't even notice Hannah going into her house until the screen door banged shut as she returned.

She had a book in her hand.

"Okay. So, I know this is crazy, but not only do I feel terrible, I want to help you fix William."

"Hannah. Look." Janelle held her palms over William. "It took me almost nine months to build him. Even if you help, we don't have enough time before the fair."

Hannah bit her lip. "'Kay, so I get that. But what about this?" She held up a page in *The Book of Unicorns, Myths, Mysteries and Magic*.

Janelle tilted her head. "Did I give you brain damage in that fight?"

"Probably, but what the hell? Let's at least try."

"Only a maiden true of virtue and heart can bring a unicorn to life."

"So, clearly *you* need to do the spell."

Janelle hugged William's cool metal frame.

"C'mon, Janelle. Just try. The worst thing that happens is it doesn't work and your sculpture is still a mess."

"All right, give me the book."

As soon as her hand touched the page, the air seemed to warm all around them.

"That was kinda creepy," Hannah said, rubbing her arms

Janelle gave her a perturbed look. "This was your idea, remember?"

"Go ahead." Hannah motioned for her to get on with it.

"Breezes blow and moonlight hovers. Hoofs of ivory dance and gallop. And true love's song brings forth the magic," Janelle sang. Her voice floated through the night, seeping into the spring flowers, the moist grass, and William.

* * *

"Well, holy shit, Janelle. You did it!"

William the Unicorn whinnied and swung his majestic head from side to side. The lawn seemed to tremble as he stood and grappled at the earth with his sinewy legs.

"Whoa." Janelle stood frozen. "*Uh*, Hannah? Now what do we do?"

Hannah rounded behind Janelle in awe of the beautiful creature. "*Um*...I don't know. I totally didn't think it would work."

"It did though!"

Suddenly, William swung his head toward Janelle, his big, round blue eyes shining. His lashes, thick and glossy black, fluttered. Janelle felt his happiness sear though her heart.

Might I suggest a ride this beautiful night? His voice rang through her mind, melodic and masculine at the same time.

"Janelle?" Hannah pinched her brows. "He's, like, talking to you, isn't he?"

"Yeah…," Janelle whispered. "He wants us to go for a ride."

"So, what are we waiting for?" Hannah squealed in delight as William the Unicorn bent down and allowed the reunited friends to climb his smooth white back.

Janelle was shaking. "I can't believe this is happening, Hannah."

Hannah reached her arms around Janelle's waist to grab a bit of William's mane. "You deserve this. And I'm sorry again for everything. Not just what I did to William tonight, but for all the years of being mean to you."

Janelle lightly kicked her heels and William took off at a slow trot, eliciting heartfelt shrieks of delight from the young women.

The unicorn romped through the shores of Schwanz Lake, then bounded through the back woods surrounding Janelle's home. The night air swirled around them, scented with budding blossoms and spring grass.

They were giddy abroad William's strong back. He trotted along, and then broke out in a gallop, evoking laughter from both the girls. But he spoke to Janelle alone, with a special inaudible language that sunk directly into her heart.

She found herself wishing that the night would never end, that she could spend her life with the wonderful, glorious creation that was William.

"*Aww.*" Hannah's yawn brought Janelle back to reality. "Girl. This has been more than awesome but we need to turn your unicorn back into a statue. Hopefully, a fully-fixed statue…"

William whinnied and shook his great mane.

Hannah patted his side. "Dude, no I didn't mean that kinda fixed."

The sun peeked over the trees, lending a soft pink glow to the water of the lake.

The dawn will take me away, my beautiful one. Thank you for giving me a night of fun and frolic. May life bring you all that you desire.

A lump formed in Janelle's throat. The magic couldn't last. She knew that. But, oh, how this creature had touched her heart in ways nobody else ever had. Or ever could.

William knelt to let the friends dismount. He glanced over his shoulder at the rising sun, bidding goodbye to Hannah with a dip of his head.

Then he nuzzled Janelle's neck, almost like a soft kiss, and gave a soft whinny of a farewell.

Golden rays of morning sun sprang up around William as he transformed back into the perfect and magnificent sculpture that Janelle had created.

Just then, Janelle heard her mother yelling. "Janelle! Are you out here?"

Janelle and Hannah looked at each other in a daze.

Carol came flailing through the lush back yard of the house toward the girls. "Oh! Here you are. I was so worried when you weren't inside." She suddenly seemed to realize that Hannah was there. "Oh. Hello, dear."

"Hi, Mrs. O'Leary."

"Well, we need to get a move on if we are to get William to the fair." Carol put her hands on her hips. "How did he get back here by the water?"

Janelle and Hannah stared at each other.

"*Uh*, we were washing him?" Hannah offered.

"With lake water?" Carol pursed her lips.

"It's, *uh*, good for the metal structure. It has, *umm*, binding molecules," Janelle said, telling her mom a little white science lie.

"If you say so. Come get some waffles and then we need to head out." Carol turned and started back, humming a tune.

The girls both stared at the beautiful sculpture.

"Wow," Janelle whispered. "Did that really happen? Did we just ride around all night on a real unicorn?"

Hannah patted the silvery metal of William's back. "Yes, we did.

And I totally vote for doing it again."

* * *

The county fair was a plethora of sights and smells. Hot dogs, cotton candy, pulled pork sandwiches, and broiled corn on the cob.

Janelle stood near William with a thousand butterflies in her stomach. She craned her neck, scanning the crowd for Marcia.

Hannah waved up from her front row seat with a grin then chomped down on another fried Oreo.

The judges walked past all the sculptures, eyeing each piece of artwork thoughtfully. A shipwreck, a giant rose, a depiction of Babe the Blue Ox…and more. There were so many talented artists that Janelle's butterflies dipped and swirled in her belly.

Oh, please don't let me throw up waffles all over the judges.

She eyed William, hoping he had heard her internal dialogue. All morning she'd been trying desperately to connect telepathically again with her magical friend, but since he had turned back into a statue there had been nothing but radio silence.

Her dream of dreams had come to life! William had given her a night to remember forever. And Hannah had totally stopped being a hag. So, no matter the outcome of the contest, it would be a great day.

The lead judge came up to the microphone. "We are proud to announce the winners of the original sculpture category."

Janelle and William were called at Purple! Janelle felt a warm rush of happiness. Her entry of William was an act of love, so to be recognized at any level was fantastic. She took the seventh place ribbon and hugged it to her chest.

It was a great achievement. Many of her competitors had been sculpting for decades. She felt wonderful and vindicated. She had dreamed of her special unicorn, William, and he'd actually come to life—in more ways than one. And even if he hadn't turned into a handsome prince, he had been enchanting.

She glanced down at Hannah, who in typical Hannah fashion was deep tongue kissing the captain of the football team. Janelle blew out a breath and stepped down the wooden stairs to greet Hannah and her tonsil playmate.

"Hey! Purple! That's so cool!" Hannah grabbed Janelle and hugged her close.

She caught sight of a green wisp of hair in her peripheral.

"Marcia!" Janelle grabbed her best friend. "Look who's here."

Marcia and Hannah stared each other down like Obama and Putin.

Carol came crashing into the picture. "Girls, girls! Oh, honey, you won purple, that's great."

Janelle hugged her mom. "Thanks. I'm really happy." She looked over at the icy-cold stare down happening between her friends. "I think we're going to go get something deep fried and celebrate. I'll get a ride home with Marcia."

"What about William?" Hannah asked.

"He stays until the fair is over. We'll bring him home Sunday night."

Hannah slanted her head toward the kissable athlete. "You guys go ahead. I'll call you. Maybe I can help you with William in a couple days." She lifted a brow conspiratorially.

As the couple walked away, Janelle said to Marcia, "You're gonna swallow a fly."

Marcia closed her mouth, opened it, and then closed it again. Finally, she muttered, "Am I in an alternate universe? Are you and that dingus dweeb friends all of a sudden?"

Janelle sighed. "I don't know. But things are way better. I've got a pretty amazing story to tell you."

* * *

The fair closed Sunday night and along with Marcia, Hannah, and her mom, Janelle loaded William into their pick-up truck and took him home to his place of honor, the middle of the front yard.

"I'd say he looks happy. Right at home," Carol said, crossing her arms and studying the tall sculpture.

"I'm going to miss him," Janelle said, looking into his big round eyes. She wished he could speak to her again. That one night where their minds met was the most exhilarating, magical feeling! He'd made her heart sing, made her feel special and loved. Of course, nothing could ever come of it. He was a unicorn, after all. He *had* come to life but not as her dream prince. He had come to life, given her something she would never forget, and healed himself so he could stand true and strong for many years.

Carol started to hum a show tune and went back into the house, leaving the girls alone.

"We have to try it again," Hannah whispered.

"I still think you both accidentally ate some bad mushrooms or something, but far be it from me to say no to magic," Marcia said. "I'm game."

Janelle pursed her lips. "I don't know. I mean, I'd love to have him back, but what if it works and someone sees us? Some scientist or zoo keeper would come steal him away."

"Oh, please." Hannah pushed Janelle's shoulder. "Your house is on fifty acres of preserve. Nobody saw us last time and nobody will now."

Reluctantly, Janelle agreed. "We have to wait until later after my mom is asleep and all the neighbors are, too."

* * *

"Try the spell again," Hannah said.

Marcia pulled her jacket tighter around her. "Maybe it's has to be, like, right at midnight or something?"

"No." Janelle set the book down. "It was eleven thirty last time. Let's face it. Maybe Hannah and I did eat bad mushrooms."

"No way!" Hannah protested. "It really did happen."

"Too bad you guys didn't get some footage with your phones. I mean, at least a couple selfies would have been good."

Hannah rolled her eyes. "You weren't here. There was no time for that. It was so amazing!"

Marcia snorted. "Yeah, you've said that now about a thousand times."

"C'mon, you guys." Janelle stood up and swallowed back the tears that were threatening. She'd tried not to get her hopes up, but she couldn't deny that she had desperately wanted a repeat of that magical evening.

Her feelings for William were as strong and true as he was.

"Maybe someday it will happen again." She brushed away a tear and tried to believe her own words.

But she didn't.

* * *

A week after graduation, the late spring breeze blew through Janelle's hair with a warmth that promised summer. The university had a pre-semester course for students with double majors and she was eager to dig in.

Dig in and concentrate on school. Look forward to the future instead of pining for William and obsessing over an event that now seemed like a dream.

The campus wasn't too busy yet and Janelle texted with Marcia while she walked.

Marcia: *Hey! How's the new campus? Did you have any classes yet?*

Janelle: *No, on my way now. Excited! Can't wait for you to come in the fall.*

Marcia: *Me too!*

Then from Hannah: *Hey, how's the new school? Any cute guys?*

Janelle: *None yet. I've only been here twenty minutes.*

Hannah: *Don't worry. I'm sure there'll be tons of hot, scholarly dudes there for you!*

Janelle grinned and shook her head. It was great having mended the proverbial fence with her old unscrupulous friend. Marcia had even warmed up to Hannah since she was no longer treating Janelle like crap.

Despite her heroic effort, her thoughts went wistfully whizzing back to the magical night with her unicorn, when she smacked right into a very solid tree.

Her phone tumbled to the ground and her backpack slipped off her shoulders, whacking the guy, who was not a tree, in the face.

"Oh my gosh!" Janelle dropped to her knees to gather up her cell. "I'm so sorry. I didn't even see you."

"*Uh*...it's okay," the stranger said, sinking to his knees as well to pick up his books. "I have to admit to texting and walking myself from time to time."

Janelle's embarrassment quickly turned to highly piqued interest. The guy was at least six foot three, and his polo shirt strained over a brawny chest. Golden highlights shone in his chestnut hair. But what caused a hitch in her breath were his eyes.

His big, round, crystal blue eyes, ringed with thick, dark lashes.

He shook his head, his wavy locks shimmering like a great mane.

Janelle swallowed, blinked, and tried desperately to think of something, *anything* to say.

The stranger blinked back, seemingly struck mute as well. Awkward silence stretched between them, along with a wonderful, fluttering, magical feeling that skimmed across their skin like the wings of a butterfly.

Janelle cleared her throat, finding her voice and her courage. "Hi. I'm Janelle."

Reaching out his hand, with a brilliant smile, he answered back.

"Hi. My name is William."

* * *

Dear reader,

This fairytale is loosely based on a true story. The sculpture of William the Unicorn is real. A former Rosemount resident, Janelle, created him when she was in high school.

One year after meeting each other in college, William proposed to Janelle on the banks of Swartz Pond in Rosemount, Minnesota. They are still happily married today and William the Unicorn stands strong and true in the front yard of Carol's home.

I want to thank Carol for sharing her daughter's story with me!

ABOUT THE AUTHOR

Peg Pierson writes paranormal comedy romance. Her first novel, *Flirting with Fangs*, is available on Amazon. She resides in the Twin Cities area where you can find her every fall haunting the register at Halloween Express!
peg@flirtingwithfangs.com
http://pegpierson.squarespace.com/

BIRDS OF A FEATHER
Dylann Crush

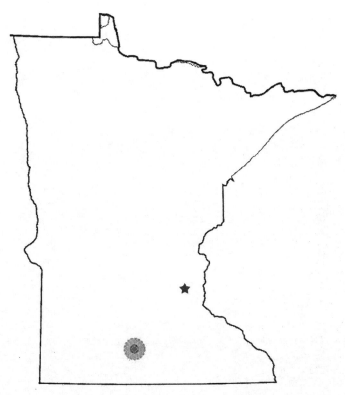

Swan Lake - Nicollet County, MN

Wren took the envelope the father of the bride passed her and pocketed it in her black dress pants. The newlyweds had just departed the reception and she was officially off duty. Mud covered her ballet flats and raindrops dotted her camera bag. Why did brides always insist on outdoor photographs? Spring in Minnesota could be so unpredictable. She shook her head as she packed up her gear. Another wedding, another freaking annoying couple of lovebirds. At least it meant another deposit into her bank account.

Being a wedding photographer had its ups and downs. Having to smile and snap photos of blissfully happy newlyweds while nursing her ailing heart had become second nature. All part of the job.

As she removed the lens from her camera and stuffed it into her bag, her cell phone rang.

"Hey, Dad. What are you up to today?"

"You won't believe what I just saw." Her father's voice shot up an octave, his excitement evidently difficult to contain.

Wren zipped up her bag. "Oh yeah? What's that?"

"My first Yellow-rumped Warbler of the season."

She smiled at his enthusiasm. "That's great. I forget, is that a big bird or a little one?" Wren never knew what to expect when her father called. An avid bird watcher, Roger was always on the hunt for a rare species or two to check off his list.

"About five or six inches. I followed him all over the park just to make sure. Your mom always said it wasn't officially spring until we saw our first butter butt."

She tucked the phone between her ear and shoulder as she broke down her tripod. "I don't care what Mom said. It can't be spring if the temp hasn't cracked fifty degrees yet."

"We're still on for this weekend, aren't we?"

"Of course. I wouldn't miss it."

"Your mother always looked forward to our spring break trips."

Bird watching was an obsession her parents had shared. As an only child, Wren had been repeatedly subjected to the forced family fun of weekend excursions to find rare species on their must-see list. But she hadn't hung a pair of binoculars around her neck in over two years. Not since the man she thought she'd spend the rest of her life with flew the coop. After Asher left, her heart wasn't in it. Less than a year after he took off, her mother passed away.

"I know. I'm sorry it won't be the same with me there instead of her, but I'm really looking forward to it, too."

Roger cleared his throat. "She always hoped you'd take up the hobby again."

"Yeah, well, don't hold your breath. I'll go with you this weekend but don't count on me to become a lifer like you."

"Don't kill an old man's dreams, all right? I'll be in touch later on this week with the details."

"Okay. Talk to you later."

"Love you, Starling."

The nickname coaxed the corners of her mouth to turn up into a grin. "Love you too, Dad."

When lung cancer took her mom, she'd never imagined her dad would want to continue the spring trips. For as long as she could remember, her parents, both high-school biology teachers in a western suburb of Minneapolis, would look forward to the break more than all of their students combined. Every year in March or April, they'd take off for some nearby bird watching hot spot and add a few more species to their list.

This year was special. Her dad wanted to return to Swan Lake, the birding watering hole he and her mom had visited on their very first adventure.

She felt bad for lying to her dad—she wasn't looking forward to the weekend, she was dreading it. Ever since her ex took off on her, Wren had avoided all things avian, especially the marshy wetland in southwestern Minnesota where she'd fallen in love. But when her dad asked her to accompany him and keep the tradition going, she'd felt obligated to say yes. As the date drew closer, a sense of anxiety sank deeper into her gut. She wasn't quite ready to face the past, but she didn't want her dad to go alone. How could she say no?

She finished packing up her gear and took the first load out to the car. With all the lights, extra lenses, and equipment, it always took her forever to break everything down. At least it had been an afternoon wedding so she'd have all evening to pull up the photos and start editing. Single and self-employed, Wren spent the vast majority of her waking hours working on her business in some capacity or another. Why would a Saturday night be any different?

* * *

The sky cast a dreary, gray tone overhead, mimicking her lackluster mood. Wren glanced over at her father as she pulled into the gravel parking lot and brought the car to a stop. Her dad peered out at the early-afternoon sky.

"You sure we're in the right place?" Wren asked.

Roger checked the map he'd picked up when they checked into the charming B&B in New Ulm that morning. "Yep. This is it."

She let out a long breath. "Okay, then. Let's get to it." She shoved her arms through her coat sleeves and pulled her mid-weight jacket up onto her shoulders. As she got out of the car, the chilly breeze blew over her cheeks.

Should have brought some mittens.

Her dad sprung out of the car, apparently energized by his close proximity to the marshlands. He cocked his head and put a hand to his ear. "Hear that?"

Wren screwed her lips into a frown and strained to carve out an individual song from the cacophonous racket. "Which one, exactly?"

Her dad closed his eyes. "It's a Sora Rail. Listen for the whinny call."

Moments passed. Neither of them said a word. The look on her dad's face warmed her heart. She'd been worried about him after her mom died. He'd thrown himself into his work—spearheading several conservation efforts and leading groups on bird watching trips abroad. Wren could only assume his trips south of the border meant he'd kept in touch with her ex, but her dad knew better than to broach that topic.

Her father had actually been the one to introduce them. He'd been on the board of the local Audubon society chapter and Asher had interviewed him as part of his doctorate coursework.

She turned her attention back to her dad. He stood at the rear of the car, rummaging through his pack.

"I brought your mom's binoculars for you to use," he said, handing her a black case.

"Oh, Dad, thanks. Feels strange to be here without her."

"She would have loved to see you back out birding. I'm glad you came."

"Me, too." As she took the well-worn binocular case from her father, the anvil resting on her heart lightened a bit.

Footsteps crunched on the gravel behind her and her dad turned.

"Hey, there, long time no see."

She'd recognize that voice anywhere. Wren took in a deep breath and spun around. There, in the flesh, all six-foot-two inches of him, stood Asher Fowler—the man who'd abandoned her. He hadn't been tempted by another woman—she would have been willing to fight for him in that case. No, he'd left her for a tiny, winged animal—an annoying eight-inch tall Carpodectes Antoniae—otherwise known as the Yellow-billed Cotinga. How could she compete with an endangered species?

They hadn't officially been talking marriage, but the topic had been broached. So, when Asher broke the news he'd taken a position in Costa Rica, she'd been crushed. The perfect combination of brains and brawn, he was loved by her parents because he could spend hours *talking* about the mating rituals of hedge sparrows. Wren loved him because he could spend hours *engaging* in the mating rituals of a horny twenty-eight-year-old and had the ability to read her like a book.

Asher's arguments from years ago rang through her ears. "It's a matter of life and death." He'd been passionate about trading in his snow gear for some sunscreen and joining the non-profit group tasked with saving the mangrove forests, the nesting ground for the endangered bird. He wanted her to go with him. She'd actually considered migrating south with him for all of about two seconds. After he left, she realized how much she missed him and reconsidered. But then her mom got sick and her life turned upside down.

"Hi, Wren." Asher opened his arms, offering a hug.

Wren turned her back to him and grabbed her camera bag. "What's he doing here?" she asked her dad.

Her father cleared his throat. "It's no secret Asher and I have kept in touch over the years. He's back in town and I knew we'd need a guide to get around the lake. He knows this place better than I ever will."

Yeah, Asher would know the area. He'd spent months researching and then writing his thesis on Swan Lake, the largest prairie pothole lake in North America. She'd accompanied him on many expeditions. The first time he told her that he loved her, they'd been dangling their feet off the dock, appreciating the fall foliage and watching the Sandhill Cranes migrate.

"Worked out pretty well, don't you think?" her dad asked.

From the corner of her eye, Wren watched Roger grab Asher's hand in both of his and pump it up and down with just a little too much enthusiasm.

"You could have warned me, Dad," she muttered under her breath.

"But then you probably wouldn't have come."

"You got that right." Wren finally turned to face the two men.

"Rog, I thought you cleared this with Wren." Asher's brow furrowed.

Wren tried not to let her gaze roam over every inch of him but failed. Her heart beat double time as she took in his durable khaki cargo pants, well-worn hikers, rugged down jacket, and knit wool cap. He'd grown out his hair, so the sandy blond strands curled over the collar of his jacket. His cheeks sported several days' worth of stubble but the honest, gray-blue eyes peering down at her were the same.

She couldn't decide what she'd rather do: wrap her hands around his neck and choke him to death for leaving her or pull his lips toward hers and take back every bad thing she'd thought about him since he'd been gone. So far, the urge to choke him was winning.

Roger shrugged. "Well, *uh*, I might not have—"

"You said you made arrangements for a guide, Dad." Wren draped the strap of the binocular case over her shoulder and set her hands on her hips. "I was expecting someone local, not a flight risk."

"Flight risk, huh? Nice touch, Wren. If you'll recall, *you're* the one who sent *me* packing. I tried calling for months—"

"I didn't want to be the one to clip your wings. Not after you made the decision to move half a world away."

"Kids!" Roger pulled out the tone he used to gain control over throngs of unruly students. "Cut it out. We're doing this in memory of Renee. Your mother"—he shot a pointed look at Wren—"would have loved seeing the two of you together for the weekend. Now, let's get our stuff out before we miss an entire day on the lake."

"I don't know, Dad. This is too much."

"I knew she wouldn't be able to handle it, Roger. Maybe it would be best if we—"

"What do you mean, I can't handle it?"

"Look, Wren"—Asher shrugged—"it wasn't fair to spring this on you. It's obvious things still aren't over for you—"

"Wait, you think I'm not over you?" Wren's jaw dropped and she snapped it shut. "I've got news for you, bird brain. I'm so over you, I've been as happy as a lark since the day you left." The lie flowed easily from her mouth though her heart seized at the attempted deception.

He wasn't buying it. Asher grinned, shook his head, and picked up his pack from the ground. "Then spending an afternoon on the lake with me shouldn't be a problem at all."

For the first time in her life, Wren found herself... speechless. Utterly and completely at a loss for words. She stood stock-still, heartbeat pounding in her ears, waiting for the perfect comeback to fly out of her mouth. It never materialized.

Convinced it was settled, Asher slung his pack onto his back. "The best bird watching is done from a canoe. I reserved one at the dock. Follow me."

Wren slammed the trunk shut and beeped her keychain to lock the car. As she trudged behind her smiling dad and smirking ex, she wondered... would it be possible to push a guy out of a canoe without tipping it over?

* * *

The rest of the afternoon passed in relative silence. Used to fully immersing themselves in a habitat, Roger and Asher engaged in minimal conversation. Every once in a while, Asher would point out a unique nesting configuration or direct their attention to a distinctive call. Wren sat in the center of the canoe and stewed.

How dare he pretend everything was smoothed over between them? *Two years go by and I'm supposed to act like he's doing me a favor by gracing us with his presence?* The one positive she could glean from the wretched day was seeing her dad fully absorbed in the setting. His eyes lit up when Asher pointed to a Pied-billed Grebe nestled in a clump of tall grass. She hadn't seen him look this happy since before her mom passed.

She pulled her hands out of her pockets and trained her camera on a black and red bird sitting on top of a cattail.

"That's a Red-winged Blackbird." Asher pointed to the subject she'd focused on as it flew away. "Means spring is here."

"Could have fooled me." Wren exhaled into her cupped hands, vowing to pick up some gloves at the Farm & Fleet in town before heading back to the B&B.

Leaning across the canoe, Asher grabbed her hands and rubbed them between his. The jolt she felt at his touch sent a cascade of shivers all the way to her toes.

"Didn't you bring any gloves?" His breath dissipated into mist.

"I was in a hurry."

"Here, take mine. I have an extra pair in my bag."

"That's okay, I'll just pick some up later."

He tilted his head down and gave her a don't-mess-with-me stare. "Put them on, Wren."

Not wanting to start another argument and wishing for warmer fingers, she shoved her hands into the over-sized thermal gloves. She'd have to take them off if she wanted to continue snapping photos, but at least they'd keep her fingers from freezing in between shots.

As Asher paddled the canoe around the perimeter of the lake, her dad put out a hand, signaling him to stop.

"What is it?" Asher held the paddle up out of the water.

Roger put a finger to his lips. "*Shh*. I heard something."

The canoe continued to glide silently through the water. A loud *tweet-tweet-tweet* sounded through the air.

"What do you think that was?" Roger asked.

"I'm not sure. Let me listen again." Asher cocked his head and a look of concentration settled over his face. "Best guess is a Prothonotary Warbler. But this is pretty far north for something like that, especially so early in the season."

Roger nodded. "That's what I thought."

"What's that? Did you see it?" A flash of yellow caught Wren's eye.

"I think we may have found ourselves a rare sighting. At least this far north." Roger scribbled a note in his pad. "Try to get a picture of it, honey."

Wren pulled the gloves off her hands and lifted the camera to peer through the viewfinder.

Asher resumed paddling, steering the canoe in the direction the yellow bird had flown. Occasionally, the *tweet-tweet-tweet* would ring out above the non-stop chatter of the other birds. But the elusive warbler failed to make another appearance.

Chilled to the bone, a few hours after they began, they returned to the dock. The sun sank low on the western horizon and strains of orange and pink bled across the sky.

Asher clambered onto the dock first and tied up the boat. He offered his hand to Roger, assisting him as he stepped out of the canoe, and then to Wren.

"I've got it," she said, refusing his help.

"You're still pissed, huh? After all this time." Asher watched her struggle with her camera bag for a moment before reaching down, grabbing her under the armpits, and hauling her up onto the dock.

"I said I had it." Wren pushed against his puffy coat, feeling the hard muscled mass of his chest beneath the layers.

"I thought you might have mellowed out a bit. Looks like I was wrong." Asher released his grip.

"I thought you were busy planting seedlings and banding birds. Why come back now?" Confused by the range of emotions racing through her, Wren attempted to squelch her curiosity and reflect a practiced indifference.

"Your dad hasn't told you, has he?" Asher brushed her hair off her face and tucked it behind her ear.

She shrugged away from his touch. "Told me what? You got sick of the sunshine and needed a fix of winter gloom?"

"Nah. He heard the Department of Natural Resources is looking to add a full-time ornithologist and he put in a good word for me. I figure I've been away long enough. It's time for me to come back to the states for good. Back to you…" his voice trailed off.

Wren's head snapped up. "Back to me? What in the hell makes you think I even want you back?"

"Wrenny, look at me." He put a finger under her chin and tipped her head up.

His gaze drilled past the layer of indifference she'd shrugged on to protect herself. Exposed, her true feelings threatened to bubble up to the surface. She looked away.

"Two years is a long time, Asher."

"I tried to come back for your mom's funeral. You wouldn't even talk to me."

"I was angry…hurt." She hadn't forgiven herself for not letting him comfort her when her mom passed. But she knew if she'd asked him to come back then he would have. She needed to know he wanted to put her first on his terms, that he wouldn't someday hold it against her if she kept him from his work. "How do you know I haven't moved on?"

"We belong together. Birds of a feather, baby. You know it. I know it. Obviously, your dad knows it. Why else do you think he invited me to come along today?"

Great, that's all she needed… her dad playing matchmaker.

"You left, Asher. You turned your back on me, on us. We had our chance. You ended it." She brushed past him, her boots clomping down the wooden dock.

As she passed her dad, she heard him ask Asher, "Where are you staying? Want to join us for dinner?"

What was Dad thinking? Wasn't spending the day with Asher bad enough? She stopped at the end of the dock and whirled around, waiting for them to end their conversation.

"I'm at the Deutsche Haus in New Ulm, same as you. I think I'll just grab something on the way back and turn in early. You still want to go out again tomorrow, right?"

Roger nodded. "I'd love to get a picture of that warbler. Let's plan on heading out right after breakfast."

"You got it." Asher pulled his pack out of the boat.

"Oh, and Asher?"

He glanced back at Roger. "Yeah?"

"Don't worry about Wren. I'll talk to her."

* * *

Wren rubbed her hands together in front of the vent, willing the cool air to warm up faster. Like hell her dad would talk to her about anything that had to do with Asher Fowler.

They drove through the compact downtown of New Ulm, with Roger pointing out the sights. He directed her to pull into a spot in front of the Kaiserhoff and treated her to an authentic German dinner of sauerkraut balls and wiener schnitzel. She washed it down with a local lager from the Schell's brewery and by the time they made it back to the bed and breakfast, Wren was ready to turn in.

"I hope you're not too upset about Asher." Roger paused outside the bedroom where he'd be staying.

"I'm not mad, Dad. I'm just…"

She struggled to find the right words to convey what it felt like to see him today. She'd given up on her own happily-ever-after when he decided to roam south. Seeing him had stirred up all kinds of feelings. Ones she thought she'd put behind her.

"It'll be fine," she said, kissing her dad on the cheek and escaping into one of his giant bear hugs.

"Goodnight, Starling. Sleep tight." Her dad kissed her forehead.

By this time tomorrow, she'd be on her way home—far away from Asher Fowler and any chance of reconciliation. How dare he assume she'd just take him back! She was finally getting over him. Had even gone on a date not that long ago. So what if the poor guy took her to a photography exhibit on birds in flight and she spent the whole time fighting back tears because it reminded her so much of her ex? She'd just have to try harder. For all she knew, Asher was just taking a break between his bird savior assignments and would take off to study the birds of the Antarctic by fall. But as she turned down the sumptuous down-filled comforter, a sliver of hope took flight in her heart. What if he really intended to stay?

* * *

The smells of coffee, bacon, and something fresh-baked and cinnamon-y woke her up the next morning. Wren hadn't been able to sleep very well; not even a dip in the whirlpool tub before bed had taken the edge off. Dreams of her and Asher and a warbling yellow bird flitted through her mind all night.

She pulled on her jeans and a sweatshirt and made her way downstairs to the dining room where breakfast was being served. Her dad sat at the head of the table, his foot propped up on the folding chair beside him and a bandage wrapped around his ankle, holding an ice pack in place.

"What's this?" Wren asked.

Roger pointed to his ankle. "Serves me right. I got up in the middle of the night to use the bathroom and didn't bother to flip on a light. It'll be all right, honey. I just twisted it."

"You should have woken me up. Are you in pain? Do you need to go to the hospital?"

"No, no. It's not bothering me at all. I'm sure it'll be fine later on today. I just need to stay off of it. Come sit down and try one of these cinnamon rolls." He gestured to the empty seat next to him.

Wren pulled out the chair and sat down. "Are you sure, Dad?"

"It's fine, really." He turned his attention back to his plate.

Before she could say another word, a young couple they'd seen at the lake the day before entered the dining room and sat down at the table.

The man leaned over and introduced himself. "Hi, I'm Matt and this is Raina."

Roger shook his hand. "I'm Roger and this is my daughter, Wren."

Everyone smiled and nodded at each other. Wren put her napkin in her lap as Ramona, the innkeeper, set an overflowing plate of food down in front of her.

"Matt and Raina got engaged last night," Ramona said.

"Congratulations!" Asher's voice boomed from the doorway as he entered the room. He shook hands with Matt and sat down in the empty seat next to Wren.

"She's a wedding photographer." Roger nodded toward Wren. "In high demand in the Cities."

"We'll need a photographer." Matt looked toward his fiancé and she nodded. "We're hoping to get married on the dock at Swan Lake in the fall."

Asher helped himself to a cup of coffee. "Leaves will be changing color. Perfect time to witness the fall migration."

"That'll be a sight," Roger agreed.

They made small talk through the rest of the meal. Asher surprised Wren when he mentioned he had put an offer down on a house not far from hers in St. Paul. He really was serious about coming back. Sitting so close to him reminded her of all those years she'd taken for granted. Dinners at her parents' house. Date nights at their favorite local Italian place, the one with the homemade meatballs. How many times had she sat next to him, assuming she'd have access to him for the rest of her life? It would be easy to fall back into their effortless routine. But how could she trust he wouldn't take off on her again?

"Care for another cinnamon roll?" Ramona asked as she refilled the coffee mug in front of Wren.

"That was absolutely delicious but I can't eat another bite." She pushed back from the table and gestured to Roger's ankle. "Doesn't look like you'll make it out in the boat today. What time do you want to head back?"

"No reason for you and Asher to miss out on another day on the water because of me. I'll just hang out around here. I was hoping you could get me a picture of that warbler if he's still flying around."

"Oh, Dad, I don't know. I think we should cancel today." No way was she going to spend the day in a boat, out on the water, alone with…

Asher got up from the table. "I think that's a great idea, Rog. I'd be happy to take Wren out to see if we can get a picture for you."

"It's settled then. I'm sure I can find a way to entertain myself for the rest of the afternoon. Go on, now."

Wren stumbled to her feet, wondering how she'd been so effectively played. *Nicely done, Dad.* She'd definitely underestimated her father. Had he even injured his ankle or was that part of his plan, too?

*　*　*

Forty-five minutes later, Wren sat huddled in the bow of the canoe as Asher paddled across the glassy surface of the water. He steered them closer to the rushes lining the shore and cocked his head, listening for the telltale *tweet-tweet-tweet* that had captured her dad's attention the day before.

"Do you really think that damn bird is out here?" Wren finally broke the silence between them.

"Sounds like it. Do you know the males pick the nesting site? Then they make a dummy nest to try to attract the females."

"Fascinating. I get the feeling my dad doesn't care as much about getting a picture of that bird as he does about you and me spending the afternoon together." There, she finally had the nerve to bring up the elephant in the room, or the albatross in the canoe.

"Roger and I have had some long talks lately."

His admission surprised her. "He does love to talk about birds."

"Not about birds, Wren. About you."

"Me? Why in the hell would you and my dad be talking about me?"

"I told you, I want to come home. Leaving you behind was the hardest thing I've ever done and the biggest mistake I've ever made."

The words she'd wished for tumbled from his mouth. How many nights had she cried herself to sleep, dreaming he'd find his way back to her?

"It took you two years to figure that out?"

He dipped the paddle into the water and the canoe glided forward. "Of course not. The first year I spent madder than hell at you for not coming with me. The next year, I threw myself into my work. But, when I finally got tired of being such a lame duck, I took a good look around and realized I'd done it to myself. Asking you to leave everything wasn't fair."

A loud honking noise came from overhead. Wren lifted her gaze to the sky, where a pair of large white birds were preparing to come in for a landing.

"Tundra Swans," Asher said. "They mate for life."

"Stupid birds. What happens when one of them gets distracted by a sexy little yellow-billed chick?"

His lips curled up in a half-grin. "That wouldn't happen. They're monogamous."

"Say some other habitat looks more appealing and the male swan leaves the female for a warmer climate?"

He shook his head. "The swan wouldn't be such a turkey."

Wren's eyes filled with tears and she wiped them away with the back of her borrowed glove. "Not even if some small bitchy bird was dying off in the mangrove forests of some faraway tropical pond?"

Asher lifted the paddle out of the water and tucked it into the boat then knelt down in front of her, causing the canoe to sway back and forth.

"I won't make the same mistake twice."

Wren gripped the sides of the canoe. "Don't rock the boat, Asher."

"Rocking the boat is exactly what I'm going to do. I love you, Wren. I was crazy to leave you and I want to come home."

Tears welled up in her eyes. "How do I know you mean it? That you're not going to rush off to Cambodia to save the Giant Ibis or track down the Bengal Florican?"

Asher's mouth quirked into a grin. "*Aw*, you remembered. I've always been partial to the endangered birds of Cambodia."

"See? I knew it!"

"Wren, I'm done chasing birds around the globe. There's only one place I ever want to be and that's with you." He reached out and took her gloved hand in his. "I told you I've been talking to your dad."

Wren nodded.

"I asked him if he'd give his permission for me to propose."

Her mouth formed an O in surprise.

He took off his gloves and pulled a jewelry box out of his

pocket. As he popped open the lid, Wren's eyes filled with tears again. Nestled into the blue velvet liner, her mother's wedding ring sparkled.

"Wren Arne, will you marry me?"

Her gaze met his and the years of anger, disappointment, and hurt melted away like the ice edging the marshy lake. His eyes glimmered with hope and the promise of hundreds of tomorrows.

Wren yanked the glove off of her left hand and let him slip her mother's ring onto her finger. "Under one condition."

"Name it. Anything, it's yours."

"You ever fly the coop again and I'll send a flock of buzzards after you."

"You got it."

Wren searched his eyes, her gaze flying over his face as he leaned in close. This was crazy, absolutely cuckoo. She barely even knew the man anymore. What if he'd changed in ways she had yet to discover? What if they were no longer compatible? What if…?

The touch of his lips against hers chased away her doubts. This was Asher…*her* Asher. All of her worry dissipated as his hands tangled in her hair. His lips parted and his tongue teased against her mouth. Eagerly, she kissed back, her need matching his.

"I love you, Wren," he murmured against her cheek.

Her breath hitched in her throat. "Love you, too, loony bird. I can't believe you. You're certifiably insane, you know that, right?"

He smiled then cocked his head. "Hear that?"

The *tweet-tweet-tweet* came from her left. Instinctively, Wren reached for the camera still hanging around her neck. She pointed it toward a rustling in the tall rushes and snapped away. A small, yellow-winged bird took flight above them, dipped toward the canoe, then shot straight up into the air and disappeared into the overcast sky.

Wren pulled the camera away and reviewed the quick shots she'd taken. "Got it. I think my dad will be pleased."

"He'll be pleased all right." Asher pulled his gloves back on.

"What about you, Wren?"

What about her? She'd started off the weekend under a cloud of dread. Now, as the sun finally broke through the dismal afternoon, a ray of light shimmered on the water next to them.

"I'd say we're off to a flying start. Now kiss me again before I have a chance to come to my senses."

Asher wrapped his arms around her. And there, in the middle of a canoe, in the center of a lake, surrounded by the riotous serenade of songbirds, Wren decided spring had officially sprung.

ABOUT THE AUTHOR

Dylann Crush writes contemporary romance with sizzle and sass. A romantic at heart, she loves her heroines spunky and her heroes super sexy. When she's not dreaming up steamy storylines, she can be found sipping a margarita and searching for the best Tex-Mex food in Minnesota.

Although she grew up in Texas, she currently lives in a suburb of Minneapolis/St. Paul with her unflappable husband, three energetic kids and a canine who doesn't think he's a dog. She loves to connect with readers, other authors and fans of tequila. You can find her at www.dylanncrush.com.

FISHING FOR LOVE
Kristy Johnson

Lake Windigo & Cass Lake - Cass Lake, MN

Tears streamed down Traci Starr's greased-stained cheeks as she struggled to get the ancient boat motor started. She had been on the dock for over an hour trying all the tricks her dad had taught her about getting the old thing running. To this point, none of them was working. Oh, how she missed her dad. Her mother passed away when she was only three years old, and her dad had never remarried. He played both mother and father to Traci, and she missed him dearly since his passing nearly four months ago.

Giving the motor a kick, she let out a string of expletives. Her anger wasn't totally directed at the old machine, much of it was directed at her so-called friends. She thought she would be able to lean on them after her disastrous breakup with Jason. She had let her guard down and talked about the situation at a party. Someone overheard her conversation and mistook it to be about someone else. Reported by the meddling party, Traci ended up accused of being judgmental and slanderous. The women then proceeded to damage Traci's reputation by perpetuating the lie.

All done with small town politics, and knowing she had to make some hard decisions about the cabin, Traci decided to spend the summer on Star Island in Cass Lake, Minnesota. This move would also put some distance between her and Jason. After her father died, he changed. A chill washed over her body at the thought of him.

Would he look for me here?

"Stupid motor! Stupid, stupid, stupid!"

"Hey, don't do that," a deep voice rumbled from behind her.

Traci, about to land another foot-shattering kick into the motor, was so startled by the sound she let out a scream. Simultaneously, she whirled around, lashing out with tiny fists against the finely chiseled, bare-chested male who had scared the living daylights out of her.

"*Whoa! Whoa*, it's okay," he said, while gently encasing her wrists, with strong, rough hands, effectively stopping the barrage on his person. "I didn't mean to scare you. I just wanted to save that motor's life."

"Let me go! Get your hands off of me!"

"If you promise to stop hitting me, I'll be glad to let go," came his impatient reply.

She struggled helplessly, desperate to pull her trapped wrists free of his grasp. He held on tightly. Once the adrenaline began to abate from her system, she relaxed. Then, realizing the absurdity of her situation, she burst into tears. She felt her wrists being released and his strong arms pulling her into his chest.

She didn't resist.

One hand gently gripped her waist and the other stroked her hair as he held her close without saying a word. As her emotions began to wane, Traci became increasingly aware of the muscular male she was pressed up against. His masculine scent. The hardness of his body. Then it hit her.

"Oh, my. I am so sorry," she said, flushing. "I'm so embarrassed."

I can't believe I just cried my eyes out on a complete stranger.

"It's all right."

She pushed herself away from him; embarrassment replaced her anger and frustration. "No, no, no, it isn't."

He looked longingly at his beached boat then at the assaulted old motor, and finally, at Traci. Extending his hand, he announced, "My name is Alex Thornton."

Sniffling and dying of embarrassment, she grasped his outstretched hand. "Nice to meet you, Alex. I'm Traci Starr."

"Pleasure to meet you, Traci Starr. Let's see what we can do about that motor."

"Do you know much about outboards?"

"Enough," he replied confidently. "Where are your tools?"

"*Umm*, I'm afraid my screwdriver is in the water and the wrench is somewhere in the boat. I have a toolbox up at the house." She paused and then continued, "You really don't need take any more time from your Saturday. I'll call a repairman. Thank you, though."

"It's no trouble, fish aren't biting anyway."

"Are you sure?"

"I'm sure. Now, about those tools?"

She looked at him uncertainly. He was a stranger. After all the tears she'd shed on his chest, she surmised she didn't need to be afraid of him. Still, she shouldn't inconvenience him further. He was offering, though, and she had no idea when she'd be able to get someone out here to fix the motor. She could be stranded out here for days without the remainder of her belongings. Sure, she had enough groceries for a few days, but she wanted her personal stuff that would turn the little cabin from a summer place into her home.

"Are you really sure?" she asked again. She wanted to be certain.

"Yes. Now, about those tools?" An edge of impatience crept into his tone.

"I'll run and get them." Smiling, she turned and started toward the cabin. Her humiliation at her outburst was lessening, replaced by an increasing desire to check her appearance. She must look affright. A few minutes with a wash rag and some cool water would surely help.

Is he watching me?

To satisfy her curiosity on the matter, she quickly turned, and received the full brunt of his crystal-blue eyes following her up the path to the cabin. Her breath caught in her throat, her face flushing as their eyes locked across the small yard. She wanted to race back and throw herself into his arms. Instead, she composed herself as much as she could, and simply shouted, "Do you need anything else?"

With an impish grin and a sparkle in his eyes, he simply responded, "Nope, just the toolbox." Then he turned his attention to the cantankerous old motor.

Happy with herself for catching him in the act of watching her, she continued to the cabin to retrieve the toolbox and freshen up.

She wanted to get back to him as soon as possible.

* * *

When Traci returned, Alex was bent over the motor, back muscles glistening in the spring sunshine. A warm heat washed over her as she took a moment to observe him work. She could watch him and those muscles all day.

Too many things to do to let a man distract me. Doesn't matter how gorgeous he is. There's a reason his last name is THOR-nton, she thought, chuckling.

Taking a deep breath, she brought the toolbox out to him. "Any progress?"

"Tell you in a minute. Is there a half-inch wrench in there?"

After shuffling a few tools around, Traci produced what she hoped was the required wrench. "Here ya go."

She didn't know why but she was disappointed when he didn't even turn around as he took it from her. He just extended a grease-covered hand and said, "Thanks."

Staring at his perfectly-sculpted backside, Traci awkwardly waited for him to ask for the next required item. She hoped he would pass judgment on the old motor soon, because she was not sure how long she could stand here watching him.

Mmm...mmm...

"Flat head screwdriver," he said, bringing her back to the dock and away from his backside.

She fumbled around in the toolbox, found the proper tool, and again placed it in his extended hand. "Here you go, doctor," she quipped.

There was a small chuckle, some sort of scraping sound, a few expletives, and a couple grunts before he stood up and looked at her quizzically. "Well, I think I found the problem. Did you disconnect anything when you were trying to start it?"

"Nope, I only did what my dad told me to do. Pump it seven times, choke it all the way, and pull. If it starts to kick in, back off on the choke, and keep following the procedure until it starts. Only I kept pulling, choking, and of course, crying."

"Yeah, I know. I was watching you."

"Watching me? Should I be worried? Are you some sort of a stalker?"

He chuckled. "I was just trying to catch some fish. You know today is the fishing opener? Right?"

"No, I didn't know that was today. Quit changing the subject."

"Me?"

"Yes, you," Traci chided. "Why were you watching me?"

"Well, while you were trying to murder that poor motor, you were swingin' that cute little ass of yours around. Made it really hard for a guy to concentrate on the fish."

Oh, girl, be careful, you could really fall for this one.

"About my motor, doctor?" she asked, feeling her cheeks flush under his gaze.

"It appears someone tampered with it. "

"What do you mean tampered with it?"

"I can't explain it but the fuel line and a couple other things were disconnected. I have them all hooked back up, though."

"Thank you so much. I really appreciate it."

"I know it's none of my business, but are you out here alone?"

Traci looked up into his face, not sure if she should answer.

What do I know about him? Other than, he's not Jason.

She stared at him a long while, reading him, judging him, determining if she could trust him. "Yes, I am out here alone, but I am not worried. I've spent most of my life out here."

"Are you sure? Maybe you should at least spend tonight in town as a precaution."

"I'll be fine. Now, how about I fix you some lunch for your services? I know a great little picnic spot on Lake Windigo. It's a little lake at the center of the island and only a short walk from here."

Alex glanced at his fishing boat, then at Traci. "Sounds perfect. I haven't been to Lake Windigo since I was a boy."

"Great, I'll go make lunch."

"Perfect, that will give me enough time to put the housing back on and get cleaned up."

* * *

Traci was just about done making lunch when she heard the roar of the old motor. She smiled at the sound. It brought back a lot of fond memories of being out here on the island, of her father. She felt safe here.

She heard the motor cut off and watched Alex walk up to the cabin, her heart rate increasing as he approached.

Wow, was he the definition of man candy or what?

"Where would you like me to clean up?" he asked, filling the doorway of the cabin.

"Bathroom is down the hall and to the left," she responded, glad that the words flowed out instead of being stuck in her throat.

"I'll only be a minute."

"Take your time."

True to his word, he was quick cleaning up and they were on their way. Traci was enjoying the silence but wanted to get to know him. See if the attraction was more than just physical. She was about to speak, but he beat her to it.

"You're pretty lucky to have a cabin out here."

"I know." She was unable to keep the emotion out of her voice. "This place has been in our family for over fifty years. There are so many memories here, so much history."

He took her hand.

They smiled at each other.

"You said you haven't been here since you were a boy. Are you from the area?"

"I grew up here in town, but I live in Minneapolis now. I've been out here before but I really don't know much about the island."

"Oh, you would be amazed at some of the history out here. There used to be a big hotel. It burned down in 1912. Star Island was also mentioned on *Ripley's Believe It Or Not* in 1958. Oh, and then there's the hauntings and other various legends."

Traci, prattling on, did not realize that Alex had stopped walking, and was caught off guard when he twirled her around into his arms and kissed her. She dropped the lunch basket, wrapped her arms around his neck, and kissed him back. She could feel his desire as she pressed her body into his. They explored each other's mouths, tasting, touching, and pressing closer together until, finally, Traci pulled back. She rested her forehead on his chest, panting, trying to catch her breath, listening to his pounding heart.

What am I doing? This is way too sudden.

Still holding her close and resting his chin on her head, Alex asked, "Do you always talk so much?"

She let out a small giggle, looked up into his blue eyes, and gave him another long, sensual kiss, before answering. "As a matter of fact, I do. Can't seem to help myself, but if it prompts you to more actions like that, I'll keep it up."

Now it was his turn to laugh.

"We best eat our lunch." She picked up the basket and grabbed his hand.

"Lead on, my lady," he said with a smile.

She gave him her best *oh brother* look and led him to the little clearing on the shore of Windigo Lake. He laid out the little blanket she had packed and they began to eat their lunch.

"I know we hardly know each other, but if you don't mind me asking, why are you out here all by yourself?"

"It's a long story."

"We have time," Alex said, as he reclined on the blanket, positioning himself so he could face her.

"You really don't want to hear all about my messy life."

"It can't be that bad."

"Yes, it can." Eyes filling with tears, she said, "I'm sorry. I'm usually not this weepy."

"It's okay. Why don't you tell me about it."

She sighed. "All right, just remember you asked for it."

"I can take it."

"Well, my dad died four months ago."

"I'm so sorry," Alex said, squeezing her hand.

Traci smiled at him. "Thank you. But that's where things get weird. My boyfriend started getting really abusive after my dad died, so I broke it off. He didn't take it well. There was a lot of talk around town. Small town politics, you know. So, I packed up my things and moved out here for the summer. I need to figure out if I can keep the place."

Pulling her down to him, he held her close, comforting her in his embrace. They lay like that for quite a while before Alex broke the silence. "What did you say the name of this lake was again?"

"Lake Windigo. I'm not sure how the lake got its name, but it's an Ojibwa term for a person who has been transformed into a monster by eating human flesh," she answered, glad for the change in subject.

"I've heard that before."

"I don't believe they live here, though."

"Really? Why not?"

Traci smiled. "Just look at this place, it's so beautiful, so peaceful. I just can't believe that anything bad could live here. I think there is another kind of Windigo, one that protects all that is good and feeds on evil."

"Kinda like a mystical superhero?"

"Exactly."

"You're so beautiful," Alex said, as he leaned in and kissed her.

Traci sat stock-still, eyes closed, breathing deeply for a long moment after Alex ended the kiss. Slowly opening her eyes, she found him staring at her.

"What?" she asked, feeling her face flush.

"Like I said, you are so beautiful."

She didn't know how to take the compliment because no one had ever told her that before, let alone made her believe it like he did. "We'd better get back, it's starting to cloud over. Looks like a storm is moving in."

"I hadn't noticed," he said, never taking his eyes off of her. "I suppose it's getting late, though. Here, let me help you up." He extended his hands to her, pulling her up off the ground and into his arms for another one of his slow, passionate kisses.

She gently pushed him away. "*Um*, yeah, we had better get going."

He smiled wryly.

She swatted him playfully. "Don't be so smug."

"I don't know what you're talking about."

"Get a move on, mister."

"Yes, ma'am."

They walked hand in hand back to the cabin and out to the beach where he had left his boat.

Standing on the water's edge, wrapped in each other's arms, and her head resting against his chest, Traci felt at peace. It had been quite a while since she had felt so at ease with someone, and she was sad to see the day end.

Sensing him hesitate, she asked, "What is it, Alex?"

"I was just wondering if it's safe for you to stay out here by yourself tonight after what happened with your boat motor."

"I'll be fine. I'm sure it was just kids messing around."

"I know you believe that, but it's still early in the season, and the other cabins are empty if you need help."

"It will be all right."

"You could come with me," he said hopefully.

Yes! He wants me. I want him. It's too soon.

"Thank you, but I am not sure that would be a good idea."

"Oh, I don't know about that"—he winked—"it sounds like a mighty fine idea to me."

"You would, but I really need to stay here. I have a lot of work to do."

He hesitated. "I can't force you to come with me. I will be back in the morning to check on you."

She lifted her head and kissed him, pulling back just a little so her hot, moist breath wafted over him. "I'd like that."

After one last embrace, he was in his boat motoring toward the other shore. Traci stayed on the beach watching him go, replaying the day, warm in the cool spring air from thoughts of him. When she could no longer hear the hum of his motor, she made her way back to the empty cabin. It was just her now. She opened the door and hit the switch to turn on the overhead light.

She froze.

In the warm glow of the cabin light, a dark shadow stood in the middle of the room.

"Welcome home, honey," snarled the figure.

"What are you doing here, Jason?" Traci demanded, hoping she had kept the fear out of her voice.

"You should have known I would come for you. Like I told you before, you're mine!"

* * *

Alex arrived back at the resort, still uneasy about leaving Traci alone on the island. Maybe he was just concerned due to the impending storm, or maybe it was because he couldn't shake the craziness of the sabotaged motor.

Or was it something more?

He had never met anyone like her. He had never fallen so hard and so soon for a woman. He was tying up the boat when he overheard two women on the beach. They were having a bonfire and chatting nosily. He figured they'd been drinking by the way they were acting, but he froze when he heard the blonde one say, "I can't believe Jason wanted us to take him to the island today."

"I think it's so romantic," the other one slurred. "Traci doesn't deserve him. She always gets the good stuff. I hate her!"

"Are you talking about Traci Starr?" Alex demanded, as he stood towering above the two women. His angry face mimicked the dark ominous clouds moving in.

"Y-y-yes," one of them stammered. "We just dropped Jason, her ex-boyfriend, off on the island. He wants to talk with her alone so she can't go running off on him again. He wants to make amends. You know, get back together?"

"He's out there now?" Alex shouted.

"Yes," they both cried.

"Shit!" exclaimed Alex, running toward the lodge. He burst through the door, startling the owner.

"Phone!" he demanded.

"Sure thing, Alex. What's up?" the owner asked, as he handed him the cordless phone.

Alex snatched the phone out of the poor man's hand. "There's an emergency on Star Island. I need Marshall." Furiously, Alex punched the numbers that would ring his friend, the sheriff.

Marshall picked up on the third ring. "Hellooo," he said, extending out the *O* in typical Minnesotan style.

Not bothering with pleasantries, he blurted, "Marshall? It's me, Alex. I have an emergency out on Star Island and I need your help."

"You do know there is a raging storm out there and the lake is covered in four-foot waves. We'll never make it."

"We have to! My friend is in trouble," Alex shouted into the phone.

"All right, Alex, we'll go. Calm down. Where are you?"

"Wishbone Resort. I'll be on the dock."

"Be there in five."

Alex slammed down the receiver and ran for the dock. He was in the process of turning the boat around when Marshall arrived.

"Thanks for coming."

"Any time, man."

"Let's get going. Hang on, it's gonna be a rough one."

The little boat bucked in the waves and a couple of times, they almost capsized. Glad for their life jackets, they were grateful when they stayed upright. Alex did not slow. Instead, he steered the boat directly toward the beach and landed it with a thud in the sand. The two men jumped out and ran to the cabin. The lights were on and Alex was hopeful that he had been wrong. That Traci would be sitting there sipping tea and watching the storm from the comfort of her living room couch. That hope was dashed when they got closer to the cabin and could see, the door swinging wildly in the wind.

"Traci! Traci!" Alex yelled, as he quickly searched the place.

Marshall, right behind him, stated the obvious. "She's not here, man."

"I know," Alex snapped, distressed.

"Do you think she's with Jason?"

"No, she'd never go with him."

"Then where is she? Where'd she go?"

Alex paused, deep in thought. "She'd go to the center of the island. She'd go to Lake Windigo. She feels safe there."

* * *

There was a bright flash of lightning followed by an ear-shattering boom. Lightning had struck very close to the little cabin. Jason was momentarily distracted by the sound. Traci, waiting for an opportunity to escape, didn't waste the moment. She bolted out the door and into the impending storm.

She could barely hear what Jason was yelling at her over the rumble of the storm; regardless of what it was, she knew it wasn't anything she wanted to hear.

Run.

Hide.

Get away.

That's what she needed to do. She thought about the boat. Alex had fixed the motor, but with the raging storm, the lake was a frothy mass of waves. She felt certain that her little craft would capsize. Then it hit her. The Lake. She had to get to Windigo Lake.

She ran.

The wind whipped her hair and the cold raindrops of spring burned her skin, but she kept running for her life. Away from Jason. Funny, her running from a psycho named Jason on a dark and stormy night. These types of things only happened in horror movies. A horror movie that completely described her relationship with

Jason. She had broken up with him out of fear. Now, she was just plain terrified.

She was close to the lake when he tackled her from behind, falling face first into the sand.

Traci screamed. Kicking and bucking, she tried to dislodge Jason from her back. "Get off me!"

"Not until you listen to me," Jason yelled, working to get Traci turned over.

The two were rolling around on the shore of Lake Windigo, Traci desperately trying to get away. Finally, one of her kicks landed on something vital. He grunted with the impact. She was able to get her feet under her, but before she could make a step, Jason caught one of her feet and pulled her down again. She fell with a thud, hitting her head. It stunned her for a moment, giving Jason enough time to gain the upper hand, pinning her to the ground.

"Get off me!" she demanded.

"Not until you admit that you're mine!" Straddling her, he grabbed her wrists with one hand, restraining them above her head.

"Never," she seethed, spitting in his face.

He slapped her with his free hand and allowed all his weight to crush the wind out of her. "I have all the time in the world to make you understand we're meant to be together."

Struggling for breath, Traci began to thrash wildly.

Do not pass out. Breathe!

He slapped her again.

Hard.

She tasted blood.

Then he was gone.

Traci, the weight of him lifted, could breathe more easily. She heard Alex roar something unintelligible. Turning over on her knees, desperately trying to catch her breath, she watched Alex hold Jason by the collar with one hand and punch him in the face with the other. Jason, desperately trying to break free of Alex's grip, was digging his fingers into Alex's hand, grabbing several digits and bending them backward, forcing Alex to release him.

Once freed from Alex's grasp, Jason quickly landed several punches to the larger man's midsection, followed by an uppercut to the jaw. Alex sidestepped, evading the fist coming toward his face, blocked, sidestepped, and then landed one of his own hits into Jason's ribs. The men continued to punch, kick, and grapple down the beach, and into the dark inky water of Lake Windigo.

Traci, distracted by the two men in front of her fighting, nearly jumped out of her skin when a hand touch her shoulder. "Are you okay? My name is Marshall. I am a friend of Alex's. You can relax, I'm the local sheriff."

"I'll live," she managed to mutter between gasps.

"Stay here," he ordered, pulling his gun and shouting, "Alex, stop before you kill him."

Amazingly, Marshall's voice cut through Alex's rage. Alex let go of Jason's shirt as he delivered one last uppercut. Jason flew backward, landing on his back in the water, the big splash barely audible in the pounding rain.

Alex quickly moved to Traci's side. "Are you okay?"

She smiled meekly up at him. "Much better now."

Helping her up and into his arms, he murmured soothingly against her hair, "I got you."

"Ain't that sweet!"

They all turned to stare at Jason as he regained his footing and stood knee deep in the lake, yelling at them. *How surreal*, thought Traci. Here they were during the middle of a raging thunderstorm, standing in the sand, soaking wet, while a crazy man shouted at them from the water. There were just no words.

"Come on out of there," commanded Marshall. "You're under arrest."

"You're gonna have to come in and get me," countered Jason.

"Why do they all want to do this the hard way?" Marshall muttered, as he made his way toward Jason. He only made it a few steps when Jason's tone changed and froze him to the spot.

"Help me! There's something in the water with me," he screamed, running for the shore.

Those were the last words Jason ever spoke.

Traci watched in horror as a massive, dark shape encompassed Jason. It blocked out the raging storm. Water ran off of it. Black as night, no specific shape. Just blackness. Then, just as quickly as it had appeared, it was gone.

Gone *with* Jason.

Traci, Alex, and Marshall looked at each other in stunned disbelief. It felt like hours that they stood in the rain, watching the spot where Jason had disappeared, but in reality, it was only minutes. Traci wished she felt sorrow for Jason, but there was only relief. He could not hurt her anymore.

She was free.

"I'll organize a search party as soon as the storm has passed," Marshall said, once their shock ebbed away.

Alex and Traci nodded mutely.

"I guess you were right, the Windigo did keep you safe," Alex finally said.

She wrapped her arms around him and squeezed. Staring at the lake, she said, "So did you."

He squeezed her back. "Always."

"All right, you two, let's get out of the rain."

"Yep," agreed Alex, looking mischievously at Traci. "It sure would be nice to get out these wet things."

"Oh, brother," said Marshall sarcastically. "You sure have it bad."

"I bet this wasn't what you had in mind this morning when you went fishing," Traci said, laughing.

"Nope. I was planning on catching some fish, not fishing for love," he said, pulling her in for a long passionate kiss.

ABOUT THE AUTHOR

Kristy Johnson grew up in Bemidji, Minnesota, attended college at Bemidji State University. Graduating with a Bachelor's degree in Chemistry and a biology minor. After graduation she married and move to Lakeville Minnesota, and now resides in Jordan, Minnesota, with her husband, two boys, two dogs and fourteen chickens.

Fishing for Love, is Kristy's fourth short story to be published in a group anthology and she is working hard to have her first full novel published in 2017.

When not writing, Kristy can be found taking photos for her company Fotonic Images, LLC, which specializes in a wide variety of photography, including portrait, sports, event and fine art photography.

To learn more about Kristy and her publications you can visit her at:

www.WildhorsePublications.com
www.facebook.com/WildhorsePublications
www.amazon.com/author/KristyJohnson
www.twitter.com/FotonicImages
www.FotonicImages.com
www.facebook.com/FotonicImages
Google + FotonicImages & WildHorsePublications
www.Pinterest.com/Outdoorgirl45
www.Instagram/FotonicImages
www.Tumbler/FotonicImages

IN THE MOONLIGHT
Katie Curtis

Lake Sagatagan - Collegeville, MN

Anna dropped her overnight bag onto the polished floor and tried to calm her erratic heart. Or at least keep the panic from her face. No luck.

"Is something the matter, miss?" the kind monk asked, gray hair the same color as his thin sweater. She only knew his religious stature because of the nametag pinned askew to his chest, plus most of the men here were Brothers.

"No, nothing's wrong." Anna shakily signed her name in the next blank spot marked *Guest*. Right under the name Luke McCarthy. *AKA my ex and the only man who knows what I look like during the full moon.*

After check-in, she followed the monk to her guest room at the aptly named Guest House, which overlooked Sagatagan Lake at Saint John's University. Not even bothering to admire the view, she dropped her things onto the bed and sped from the modern glass and steel retreat center. The all-male campus was situated on the shoreline of the large lake and dated back to the 1800s. It shared academic esteem with its sibling school, the all-female College of Saint Benedict, which rested a few miles down the interstate in the middle of cornfields.

It shouldn't have surprised her to see Luke's name in the guest book. She'd known he'd be there, along with thousands of her old St. Ben's and St. John's classmates. They had been cordially invited to give the welcoming address at the ten-year reunion—just the two of them. The request to speak came on the heels of her latest publication in *New Scientist*, a popular UK-based science magazine. Of course she'd said yes! But then to find out the only other guest speaker was Luke McCarthy, legendary star kicker for Alaska's football team, the Malamutes. The only man—and she used the term loosely—to never miss a kick in his entire professional football career?

God, she'd wanted to back out. It was too late and she was stuck, waiting with thinly veiled apprehension to share a podium with the one man who could ruin her entire existence.

A cool spring breeze raced up from the wide lake and she ducked into the Great Hall, even though she rarely felt the cold.

The Great Hall hadn't changed in ten years, or a lot longer judging by the degree of dust that clung to the overhead banners. The balcony-lined room had once been the Chapel for St. John's University, a beautiful testament to the artisans who had created such a vibrant and historic campus. Rich wall paintings stretched across the curved backdrop of the old altar, and at Christmas, a huge tree was brought inside and decorated. The ceiling was low compared to most churches, but it still rose two stories with upper stained glass windows to catch rays of sunlight.

There was a solemnity in entering the Great Hall, a sense of awed quiet, and Anna loved it. She'd spent hours curled up with a good book in one of the scattered old chairs, coffee from the Java by her side and nothing but the calm creaking of the brick building to keep her company.

Her nose, more sensitive than a human's, picked up an underlying mustiness, common in a brick building that had survived decades of harsh Minnesota winters, as well as the crisp scent of fresh linens and silver polish. As well as an underlay of spice that reminded her of—*Nope, don't think about him. Don't do it!*

"Takes you back, doesn't it?" Luke spoke over her right shoulder, his quiet voice still managing to echo. Her heart sputtered and she twisted around to glare at her ex.

"How is it you always manage to sneak up on me?"

"I'm quiet as a church mouse," Luke said.

Cue the eye roll. "*Uh-huh*, it has nothing to do with the fact you love scaring the shi—*crap* out of me?"

"Oh, wipe the look of eternal suffering from your face and admit you missed me." He stepped far too close and she was forced to crane her head back to keep her gaze on Luke's baby blues.

They glared at each other for several tense minutes, each refusing to back down. Anna geared up for a long dry-eyed, old-fashioned staring contest when he surprised her by looking away, over her shoulder. A sign of respect for a creature like her.

"That would involve lying, and I never lie," she blurted. "Honesty's the best policy, you know." She winced. What was it about Luke that had her blubbering like a schoolgirl every time he was within smelling distance?

Uh, probably because he smells like salted caramel and warm spice?

Luke ruffled her dark hair with a wide palm and smiled his stupid lady-killer smile.

She sighed. "You haven't changed a bit."

Luke still possessed the same cocksure stance, narrow hips, and wide shoulders that made a woman want to climb him like a jungle gym. He'd been a football player at St. John's, a good one, too. It wasn't until after the "incident" during their sophomore year, though, that he'd become the best player the Division III school had ever seen.

"I'd like to think I've bulked up compared to the scrawny young man you knew." He smirked, thick biceps stretching the bands of his plain white tee and muscled thighs shifting in his worn jeans, which were no doubt more expensive than her entire outfit.

"You were such a string bean back then. I was amazed your pants stayed up."

"They were down around my ankles more times than not." Luke winked.

"That's not what I meant," she said as a hot blush crept up her cheeks. Easily, she recalled many a time when his pants had been in a heap on her dorm floor.

"I know. It's fun to tease you." He ran his fingers through his short, dark hair and looked around as if seeing the hall for the first time. "You live for so long with only memories as a guide, but I'd never forget this place, or that one spot on the drive up."

IN THE MOONLIGHT

Anna stepped away from his intoxicating scent and flopped into an open chair. Memories from that particular night ran through her mind. God, if she closed her eyes she could still hear the screams.

"Sorry, I didn't mean to bring it up." He cursed and shoved his hands into the front pockets of his denim. Surprisingly, he colored and glared at the floor. "Dammit, Anna, I swear I practiced this speech a thousand times on the plane and not once was I going to bring that night up."

She tucked her fingers between the legs of her jeans and rubbed them together for warmth. Just a mention of the "incident" and goosebumps broke out over her skin, chilling her to the bone in a way arctic gusts never could. "We might as well talk about it."

Truth be told, it had been on her mind since she'd realized he'd be speaking too. There was no way to avoid it. When a person experienced something so life-altering they questioned their very existence, it was hard not to think about it all the time. And then to share such an encounter with someone else?

"Good, it's been a long time coming," he said.

A group of students wandered in, backpacks slung over their shoulders and more than half wearing plaid. She snorted, having forgotten about "Flannel Fridays." Luke ducked his head and made a beeline for Anna. He grabbed her elbow and dragged her out of the Great Hall.

"Oh shit! Are you Luke McCarthy?"

Too late. She winced.

"Guys! I told you it was him!"

The pack of students swarmed Luke and it took twenty minutes for him to break away. Anna sat back and took in the man he'd become. No longer was he the gawky freshman who'd taken her breath away on a walk home one spring evening after they'd bumped into each other post-party. He'd been such a gentleman.

And then, she'd jumped his bones like an overeager young woman intent on discovering her own sexuality. She grinned at the memory. It had been a wild thing between them, like the poles of a magnet finding each other for the first time, compelling and intense.

But then one night at the beginning of sophomore year, coming home from another party, she had been attacked. Luke had ran back to the party to grab her sweater, for a few moments, she'd been alone. Luke fought so hard to protect her, he'd broken several ribs and suffered a bad concussion. Their assailant fled into the night.

"You're thinking about it, aren't you?" Luke escaped the group and walked with her down a winding driveway to the lakeshore. Spring blossoms twirled in the trees and the pleasant scent of freshly-turned earth fluttered in on the wind.

"Yeah, I take one look at your face and it all comes tumbling back." The fear was still there. "I still have nightmares of screaming for help as that thing mauled me, of scrambling into the street down at Flynntown, hoping one of the senior boys would save me. And there you were, running in like Hell and taking the brunt of my beating."

"Some goddamn knight I was." He hung his head and flung a rock into the water. "The lupine had already bitten you."

"You saved my life at the cost of carrying the virus." Anna hugged herself for warmth. "We both turned into rabid beasts."

"Rabid beasts with really cool superpowers."

"Don't you think it's cheating? Using your 'special-ness' to get ahead?"

"Like you didn't use yours? Hello, pot, meet kettle." Luke shook his head, looking annoyed. "How many all-nighters did you pull doing your post-graduate work and had no ill effects? I bet you could go three days without sleep and maybe need an espresso, at the most. You had time on your side, the ability to intensely focus and tackle your problems like a predator going after weak prey." He stormed a few feet away. "Don't act all high and mighty with me, Anna. Don't you dare, you of all people."

She had the grace to duck her head. It was true, she'd used her abilities shamelessly in grad school, single-handedly holding down three jobs and acing her courses because she could. She rarely slept more than two hours a night and possessed a stamina that would make marathon runners jealous. She'd graduated with honors because she was smart, but yeah, she'd used every trick in the book to get ahead of her classmates. In record time, she'd earned her doctorate in animal physiology and the clout to travel the world and learn more about her "affliction."

The lupine pathogen had transformed her body in ways she was still discovering. It had taken her two years post-incident to realize her memory had vastly improved.

"Goddammit, Anna, I gave up *so much*." Luke sighed. "I had to switch positions and spend every second of my professional career holding back in order to keep my teammates and opponents safe. It was either follow my dream or sit in a cubicle and slowly die. I cut out my family because they didn't understand why I couldn't come for holidays that fell on the full moon. Couldn't have a normal relationship.

"Because the second I felt comfortable with someone, the full moon rolled around and I hurt them emotionally by keeping my distance. Or had to dull my reactions to normal fun things like sex because of the fear of hurting them," he said.

Anna yanked her hair over her shoulder. "Yeah, I get it, life got fucked up. But we learn to deal, it's what defines our character."

"Which is why we should be together."

"Why?" she asked, incredulous. He'd said shit like this all the time in school, but she'd broken up with him when she realized what they were. Being together and reliving that torture would have crippled their lives.

"What if we're the only ones of our kind?"

"Like a 'last man on earth' situation?" She balked, not hiding the disgust on her face. "Trust me, Luke, I wouldn't marry you even if you *were* the last of my kind on earth."

"Ouch." He clutched his chest in mock pain. "Want your knife back?"

"God, that's not what I meant. I'm sorry." Anna shifted her

sandaled feet in the sand. "I didn't want to hurt you, especially after what you did for me. But I didn't want to hold you back. I refused to let you be my comfort zone. We needed to go live and relearn normal."

Luke pasted a half-smile on his handsome face and slung an arm around her shoulders. "Look where it got us. Right back where we started."

"Where is that?"

"Together."

They'd stayed silent on the walk back to Guest House, going their separate ways for dinner, but his words kept playing in her head. They had fruitful careers and, at thirty-one she was proud of the breakthroughs she'd discovered, and Luke was a year away from retirement from football. What was next for them?

Could we be normal, together?

* * *

The beginning swell of the moon peeked over the treetops and her skin burned, stretched tight over shifting bones. A thunderous crack exploded from her spine and she fell to her knees in the middle of the woods, a plain black tee stuffed into her mouth to muffle the sounds of her screams. Pain burst between her shoulder blades as she dipped forward onto all fours, itchy palms finding her discarded jeans.

Need the syringe. Her eyes rolled back in her head with the next spasm. She hadn't meant to take so long but she'd been rewriting her speech for the ninth time and hadn't realized how late the hour had grown. Trimmed nail beds elongated into razor-sharp claws, and she accidently shredded the left hip of her jeans while searching for her medication.

"Heard you changing. Had to come. Helpless." Luke staggered out from behind a thick oak trunk. It was the second time in one day he'd caught the drop on her.

Only now, she was stark naked on all fours in the middle of the woods with a shirt wedged between her bulging jaws. He, too, was without a shirt, and as the moon shifted from behind a budding branch, he swore and dropped to the ground.

Her back arched and she lost sight of him as her own change came upon her. Screams burst from her mouth when her ribs shattered as sinew and muscle reknitted itself into a frightening shape. *Hurts so bad.* The spasm shot through her and she could breathe again.

Looking up, she saw Luke on his back, legs in the air as he kicked off his jeans while a wave of the change slammed into him. Fur sprouted along his bare abdomen and shot down his naked legs. Anna knew how terrible the change was, she experienced it every month, but she hadn't seen another person go through it in ten years.

It was worse to watch someone's kneecaps crack and break so the angle of the lower legs could point the opposite direction, than to experience it. Too late for her special homemade remedy, she took a deep breath in with her nose and let the metamorphosis roll over her like a wave on the beach.

Once she stopped fighting it, the rest of the shapeshifting lasted no more than thirty seconds. An eternity when all of your bones broke and every muscle switched places. The ability to think turned murky and sensations bombarded her mind. Anna the human was no more. In her place was a wolf as big as a Newfoundland, weighing a lean one-fifty. Her pelt was a soft auburn and chestnut, her paws as big as bagels.

Before her stood the largest wolf she'd ever seen. The beast in her growled in greeting and dug at the earth between them. A black wolf as big as a mule sat on its haunches and canted its shaggy head at her, golden eyes shifted over her bunched muscles. Without meaning to, her wolf took the reins and rolled onto her back to expose her belly to Luke.

Inwardly, she fought against the submissive pose. But, as with all animals, there was a respected hierarchy in which Luke was the alpha, and for her to behave otherwise would have given him permission to attack. She might as well have been a pup in comparison. His pointed snout sniffed at all her good bits before bumping her shoulder good-naturedly.

She flipped back onto her legs, and they circled each other and sniffed repeatedly, her senses on alert. She smelled no aggression, only the pleasant aroma of spring breaking through fresh dirt and male interest. She snorted and took off running. Luke bayed and she heard him race after her.

They pounded through the forest in perfect harmony. For hours, paws hit the earth in silent sprays of dirt. Nothing compared to sprinting after prey. She rejoiced at the companionship and tackled Luke after they'd taken down a doe. The male wolf let her play-wrestle, but then he flipped her onto her back and pressed a heavy paw to her chest, a rough tongue hanging out as he panted.

Luke twitched an ear to the south. She cocked her head from her upside-down vantage point and listened.

Kaboom!

The sound of a rifle shattered the night air. Men's voices followed the gunshot. She swore in her head. The two of them had not been quiet and baying wolves were bound to get noticed up in farm country.

Luke let her up and hunched low, weight braced on all legs as he growled in the direction of the gun. If they were caught, it would be nothing but science labs and news specials for the rest of their lives.

Anna bounded in front of Luke and dropped down on all fours to belly crawl in submission to his front legs. She licked his paw to gain his attention. Then, in a bold move that might get her injured, she bounced up and hit him in the shoulder. The move hadn't been anticipated and the black wolf tipped over, his weight unbalanced.

With him incapacitated, she took off running back toward Guest House. They wouldn't switch back to human form until dawn and this far from civilization, there was a good chance those hunters would find them. They'd left a bloody deer carcass nearby. Wolves usually stayed away from bright lights and homes. They'd be relatively safe from discovery in the woods bordering the beach, leaving the hunters or farmers to search the deep woods all night long.

A male wolf couldn't resist a running female and sure enough, she heard the sounds of Luke chasing after her. Anna slipped through the trees as a silent shadow and padded up the steep hillside to the edge of the Guest House. Her room faced the lake on the first floor and she'd escaped out her window, leaving it cracked so she could reenter in the morning without alerting the staff of her nighttime wandering.

She nudged the edge of the windowpane with her nose and used her rock-hard skull to jimmy the glass upward until even Luke's large frame could creep in. He caught up to her, a warm wall of male wolf leaning into her side. They both slipped into the Guest House through her window, two dark beasts curling up with the sheep.

* * *

Anna bolted upright. She'd had the worst nightmare. In it, she'd been unable to use her syringe to temper her morphing into a furry beast under the light of the moon and had ended up running wild and killing a deer. With Luke McCarthy at her side.

Blinking away sleep, her eyes adjusted to the bright light of her rented room. No sign of Luke. Thank God. She was naked under the thin sheet with only fuzzy memories of last night. Her serum should have cleared the fog already so she'd be able to remember what she did in beast form but for some reason, it wasn't working.

Which didn't make sense. Obviously, she'd walked into the woods and plunged the syringe—*oh no!* She hadn't been able to get into the tight pocket of the jeans with her clunky claws and…and…*Luke had shown up*. It hadn't been a nightmare

As if reading her mind, the male in question slung a jean clad leg over the threshold of the open window, holding the remains of their clothing in his arms. He looked up and saw her staring, his gaze fixing pointedly on what she hid with the threadbare sheet.

"Listen, Luke, last night was a mistake. I was supposed to take my serum but I couldn't get to it. And I normally don't go gallivanting through the forest looking for deer…" She trailed off when he lifted her unbroken syringe and set it on the nightstand. "What did we do last night? Other than the deer?"

"It was always just a matter of time. You and me, baby." He winked. She rolled her eyes. "Relax, you curled up like a lamb the second we got in and I slept on the floor like the gentlemanly wolf I am. You know, you keep saying 'no' and a guy's pride is bound to get wounded."

"I wish," she muttered.

If he heard her, Luke ignored the comment. They sat in silence for some time, watching a trio of squirrels zip about tree trunks with uncanny speed out her window. Fluffy tails whipped up and down as the rodents scampered along the forested path to the shore. She grinned, thinking of her own fluffy tail.

"I'm glad you said no." Luke stood and tugged his muddy white tee over muscles that had her drooling. *In my dreams.* "To dating me again after what happened to us."

"We needed time to adjust to what we were, what we are." Anna tugged the sheet tighter and frowned. "Can you imagine if I'd said yes? We would have been wholly dependent on one another, never branching out, never seeking other relationships."

"We never would have achieved normal," Luke said.

"Have we really, though?" Anna stared past him out the window at the budding treetops and the glassy surface of the lake. "Look at us. I'm a woman with a Doctorate degree in animal physiology currently embroiled in studies that are borderline Frankenstein-ish, creating my own serums to dampen my lupine abilities. Then there's you, an athlete who has to visibly hold back every time he plays so as not to arouse suspicion or hurt his team members."

"I'd say we're normal enough, under the circumstances." Luke set her folded clothes on the edge of the bed and moved to the doorway where he paused. "Besides, normal is overrated."

He walked out.

Anna spent the rest of the morning showering off the evidence of last night. Then she dressed in a pencil skirt and matching white blouse before wolfing down a hearty breakfast of bacon, eggs, and pancakes. Speeches started at eleven, followed by a luncheon, and then there were programs throughout the day, dinner on your own, and a formal dance to end the festivities. She planned to avoid Luke and her feelings toward the alpha wolf through all of it.

The plan worked great. Not only did her speech on what it meant to be a St. Ben's alum blow away her classmates—it even elicited a standing ovation—but she'd been able to introduce Luke with only a minor blush.

Her day was spent bonding with people she hadn't seen in a decade and growing transfixed by every wave of Luke's sinewy forearms, and every flash of his baby blue eyes. He wasn't shy about meeting her gaze and winking.

She didn't want to feel this way about him, about any guy. With an "affliction" like hers, she'd learned to keep people at a distance. But everything was different with Luke. Not only did he already know her secret, but he had the same skeleton in his closet.

Finally, after a quick dinner with some of her old roommates, Anna slipped into a slinky black dress and matching high heels sure to break a normal girl's ankles. She planned to briefly show her face at the dance before she'd have to make her exit. All too soon, the sun would set and the moon's power over her would win. Getting furry at her ten-year reunion wasn't what she had in mind for a killer exit.

She was chatting up an old guy friend when a calloused hand slid along her elbow. *Luke.* His warm spice and salted caramel scent rolled over her and she leaned into his touch. Her friend waved and left, giving Luke the chance to pull her into the shadows of the room.

"Wanna get away?" he asked.

"Yeah, I'm feelin' itchy already."

She led the way out of the makeshift ballroom, down the dark hall and outside. She leaned against the cool stone building to battle the heat erupting inside her body. Luke stepped in close.

"Do you regret what you did?"

He raised a brow at her blurted question. "I'm to assume you mean the 'incident'? Yeah, I regret you had to experience pain and the loser got away with it. Do I regret stepping in and saving you? Never. If anything, I'm grateful I stepped in because now there's a bond between us nothing can break. Because you and I are of the same cloth."

The conviction in his voice sealed it for her. In the back of her mind, she'd always wondered if he played nice because she'd been a damsel in distress, or if he'd hated her for the outcome of his Good Samaritan routine.

"I think we should, ya know, *be together*," Luke said, eyes glinting in the light of the street lamps.

Her heart fluttered and she knew he heard it. More than anything she wanted to believe he wanted her for her, so she asked the hard questions. "Why? Just because we share a traumatic experience? Or because we're Lupine, and alone in the world?"

"Of course, yes. But maybe it's all three. Our lives were irrevocably altered that night. Who else in the world would understand our motivations? Our experiences? Our drives? Who else would race into the moonlight with you? Who else would hold their head back and howl at the night sky at your side?" He stepped even closer, their lower bodies meshing together. The now-familiar feeling of falling hit her.

A wicked smile lit Luke's face. He leaned into her and brushed rough stubble along her nape. It tickled. "Who else would lick the blood from your muzzle?"

The memory of them together in wolf form, thick fur wavering in a chilly breeze, a kill at their feet, and him nuzzling her damp nose, made her spine tingle. It shouldn't have excited her. If she were anything other than lupine, it would have grossed her out. The knowledge that he wanted to hunt with her, that this alpha male would tend to her needs…it was as much an admission of love as anything.

Her heart clenched and she wanted to do it all over again, tonight and every night of the full moon. *So why not? Why not just say yes?* A yes to Luke McCarthy was like jumping feet first into a black hole—no way out. Damn if it didn't make her giddy.

"Race you to the chapel!" She slipped off her heels and bolted for the shoreline. The rumble of Luke's laughter followed as she sprinted past ivy covered stone buildings on the way to the beach.

* * *

Warm spring sunshine beat down on her bare legs as she dangled them over the edge of the ledge that acted as a railing for the short stone steps. Luke rustled around in the little chapel, no doubt searching for his shoes.

A blush crept over her cheeks as Anna replayed in vivid detail the very "hands-on" way Luke woke her this morning. Not once was it necessary for her to hold back as they'd rolled around the makeshift pallet of clothes and screwed the ever-living daylights out of one another. In a chapel.

Smite me, God. Hashtag, worth it.

"Was I right, or was I right?" Luke stepped out into the sunshine as he finished buttoning a pair of buttery soft jeans. "Sex with a lupine blew your friggin' mind."

"Cocky asshole." She spun around on the ledge to face him and grinned like a cat that'd found a stash of catnip. Only she was a lupine who'd found the world's biggest chew toy. "But yes, you were right. God, I don't know how I'll go back to mundane human sex. Stamina's just not the same."

Luke's smile sent little butterflies to her belly and her bare toes curled. He stepped up to the ledge, hands on either side of her hips to brace him and trap her in the cocoon of his embrace. "As if you'd ever have the chance to go back to 'mundane human sex.'"

She raised a brow. *Oh, I wouldn't, would I?*

"The only reason I accepted this stupid chance to speak was because I knew you were speaking too. This was my one chance to not fuck it up. Dammit, woman, I've been drumming up the courage to see you again ever since we graduated." He ran his fingers through his hair while the muscles of his chest flexed and rippled with the movement.

Her heart was in her throat as he gazed down at her with those iconic baby blues. "Me too. I mean, I've been sort of avoiding you but not because of me not liking you." God, her words were all jumbled. "What I'm trying to say is, you scare me, these feelings I have for you scare me. It's not just the wolf thing, because we got together before then. But…"

"So you feel it too?" he asked, hope lighting up his face. "It's like we picked right back up again from sophomore year."

She nodded past the lump in her throat. There was this wonderful, giddy sensation of falling as she looked into his expressive face. As if their relationship had hit pause due to unforeseeable circumstances, and now that they'd crossed the distance again, how could they come apart? Like opposing magnets, inexorably bonded together.

"I'm not asking for your life, Anna. I'm just asking." Luke bent down to rest the faded denim of his right knee on the dusty ground. He knelt before her, eyes crystal clear as the morning sky. "I'm asking to play a part in your future. I'm asking if you'll let me run alongside you in the moonlight for however long our lifespan is, because, I love you. I think I always have, ever since you bumped into me wearing that red hoodie and a smile way back in freshman year."

She had no words. It wasn't every day that the alpha lupine you'd been lusting after for over a decade laid his heart at your feet.

"If marriage is too antiquated an ideal for you, then fine. We won't marry. I'll just demand to wake up next to you every morning and prowl after you all day long. You might as well marry me for the tax benefits considering I'll be underfoot anyway."

Tears clouded her eyes and she lost it, great big sobs coming so fast she could barely breathe. Luke must have stood because in the next second, she felt rather than saw his broad chest press against her, arms coming around her trembling shoulders to hold her close. Her legs tangled together around his hips from her perch on the ledge.

"You hate the thought of being with me that much, huh?" There was no laughter in his voice.

God, she had to make him understand this time she wasn't saying no, but the tears kept coming. A warm hand rubbed between her shoulder blades. And she cried that much harder. *I'm not some emotional nitwit! Pull it together, Halverson!*

"Had I known a marriage proposal would make you bawl, I'd have done it in the middle of your speech. That way yours wouldn't have been so much better than mine."

She chuckled softly and dried her tears on the shirt she'd borrowed from Luke. "Still would've rocked the audience."

Luke laughed, head thrown back and shoulders shaking, and she reveled in the sound. Luke McCarthy, her freshman year crush, the only person who knew her secret, the only person she truly trusted, loved her. It'd only taken him ten years to admit it. She smiled.

"I'm not usually like this," she hiccupped. He looked down at her, face creased into a sardonic smile. "It's just all the other times you've broached this subject, it's been teasing and funny. I never dreamed you were actually serious. In answer to your monologue, if you ever get around to actually asking me to marry you, there's a good chance you'd like my answer."

Luke's brows lifted and he sucked in a breath. "Hot damn!"

Anna chuckled again as he dropped back into the usual pose, knee on the ground and hands clasped over his heart. "Anna Halverson, would you make me the happiest lupine on the face of the earth and marry me?"

She leaned down to kiss him with one word on her lips. "Yes."

The End

ABOUT THE AUTHOR

I'm a Netflix Binger, full-time job holder, word-maker-up-er, person who can't stop telling stories. I live in the northern United States where it's cold all the frickin' time and there's no pretty ocean to look at. So I write about it instead.

You can find me staring out a window (pretending to look at pretty water vistas when all I see is cracked blacktop), sipping French press coffee and listening to ocean waves, while I drown out the soccer game my husband is cheering for at full volume.

If you want to know more there is a blog, an Instagram account full of food pics, a Pinterest account where I share the inspiration for my stories, and Facebook/Twitter where I share extremely unintelligent posts.

www.katiecurtisnovelist.wix.com/home
www.pinterest.com/katiecurtisnvst/

IN THE MOONLIGHT

NOR-WAY TO LOVE
Rose Marie Meuwissen

Lake Harriet - Minneapolis, MN

Bells chimed throughout her apartment, as she made her way to the door.

"Good morning, ma'am, delivery for Sonja Thorson Miller," the man immediately announced when she poked her head through the slightly open front door. Sonja accepted the proffered clipboard and signed her name, stating she'd received the package.

Sonja saw the Norwegian postage stamps and knew immediately what was inside. She opened the large box and carefully took out the hand-sewn Telemark *bunad*, which was a traditional Norwegian folk costume. Apparently, the pictures hadn't done it justice, as it was absolutely the most beautiful dress she'd ever seen with its red floral stitching on black wool fabric. The attention to detail and stitching done by skilled and experienced hands was incredible. Her only fear about ordering the bunad online from the *Husfliden* store in Oslo was that it wouldn't fit when she got it. She walked into her bedroom and gently spread out the blouse and the bunad, with its sleeveless bodice type vest attached to a full-length black skirt, on the bed. Quickly, she removed her jeans and shirt, then put the delicately embroidered white blouse on first and slipped the bunad over her head.

Relief spread over her face as she fastened together the ornate pewter hooks. It fit perfectly. She stood in front of the mirror, looking at her reflection. Her long blonde hair fell in curls over her shoulders, highlighting her petite, slender figure as her blue eyes sparkled back at her. The picture it portrayed was definitely like one from the pages of a history book.

Mom, I hope you can see this. I know you would be proud to see me in this bunad from Norway, portraying your ancestry.

After she gently took the bunad off and hung it on a heavy-duty hanger, she lovingly put it away in her closet.

She called her dad to let him know it had arrived. He had been unenthused when she told him she was ordering it. Though, to her surprise, he said he knew about them, because her mother had often talked about the traditional folk costumes while she was still alive.

"Dad, the bunad arrived today and it is so beautiful. Can you come over to see it?" she asked.

"Sure, Sonja. I'll stop by after work tonight. I have a gift for you, too. I'll bring it along."

"Dad, you know you don't have to buy me things."

"I know I don't have to. Gotta go. See you tonight."

Sonja didn't have a clue what her dad had bought for her, since it wasn't something he usually did. She tapped her computer, bringing it to life again, and went back to work, setting up advertising pages for her clients on their websites and sending emails out to their customer lists.

* * *

At seven, her doorbell rang. Her dad, Karl, smiled brightly as she opened the door.

She leaned in to casually hug him, as he had never been the touchy-feely type of guy. "Good to see you, Dad."

"It's been a busy day today, how was yours?" he asked, as he walked inside carrying a small gift bag.

"Hectic as usual with all the normal deadlines for a Friday."

"So, where is this bunad you ordered?"

"In my bedroom, I'll get it." Sonja started to leave the room.

"Can you model it for me? I'd like to see it on you," Karl requested with a huge smile for his daughter.

"Sure, have a seat. It'll take a few minutes to put it on."

Sonja grinned as she walked away. *He wants to see it on me!* She hadn't thought he would even want to see it, much less have her model it. Well, she couldn't show it to her mother or her grandparents, so she would be more than happy to show it to her father.

"Here it is," she said, as she twirled around so he could see the full skirt in all its glory. "So, what do you think?"

"You look beautiful. I know this would've made your mother very happy. Her Norwegian heritage always meant a lot to her." He picked up the gift bag and handed it to her.

She took it from him, wondering what could possibly be inside.

"Go ahead. Open it."

She set the bag down on the table and removed the tissue paper. Inside were two jewelry type boxes. She opened the first one to find a large Norwegian *Solje* pin. She only knew what it was because she recognized it from the Husfliden's website from when she ordered the bunad. They were expensive, she knew that much.

"It's beautiful!" Sonja removed it from the box.

She fastened the two-inch silver pin adorned with hanging spoon-shaped silver pieces onto the front of her blouse, then reached inside to take the other gift out. This box was old, and when she opened it, she saw another, smaller Solje pin. She gently took it out, as it was obviously old and extremely delicate in nature.

"Dad..."

"It was your mother's." He stared at her shocked face.

"I never knew she had anything from Norway." She held it in her hand and was in awe of the pristine condition of the antique pin.

"She always wanted to get a bunad. In fact, the one you're wearing, the Telemark bunad. But at the time, we couldn't afford it. One year, her mother—your grandmother, Gunhild—bought her this Solje pin for Christmas. She wore it proudly with her Norwegian sweater."

"Oh, Dad, I can't thank you enough for holding on to it for all of these years and giving it to me now. I will treasure this forever. It is like a double treasure since grandmother bought it for mother."

"The other one is from me. I bought it for you down at the Norwegian store, Ingebretsen's, on Lake Street in Minneapolis."

"And I will treasure this one, too, since it came from you." She attached the smaller, older Solje pin below the new larger one.

"I'm so sorry, Sonja, that I deprived you of all of this. You could've spent time with your grandfather, but I was so wrapped up in my pain from losing your mother that for years I couldn't bring myself to see him. And by the time I came to terms with my loss, I felt I'd burned that bridge long before and was too afraid to try to mend it. I am so sorry, Sonja."

She reached out and hugged him. His body was shaking as he cried. "It's okay, Dad. I didn't understand when I was little, but I do understand now. There's nothing we can do about the past anymore, but we can make changes for the future."

* * *

Sonja opened her laptop and searched on the internet for Ingebretsen's, the store her dad had mentioned. They had a very informative website offering a huge selection of Norwegian and Scandinavian products for sale, as well as information about local Norwegian events.

It appeared there was still, even in this day and age, a Norwegian Lutheran Church, called *Mindekirken*, which held religious services and hosted events honoring the culture. The one celebration that caught her eye was the National Day of Norway, an official holiday in remembrance of their Constitution Day, observed on May 17th each year in Norway and America. It was commonly referred to as *Syttende Mai* and celebrated with a parade held in the streets surrounding the church. Everyone was encouraged to wear their bunads. Perfect, a place where she could finally wear the beautiful traditional folk costume. But, she felt a bit apprehensive about going alone and not knowing anyone. There was always her dad, though. Maybe now since he wanted to encourage her efforts to embrace her Norwegian heritage, he would accompany her.

* * *

"Dad, thanks for coming with me," Sonja said, before he dropped her off at the door to the church and then went to find a parking place.

They found some of the last available seats in the balcony. She was amazed to see all the colorful and different bunads. From the Husfliden's website, she knew each region had their own specific bunad and they were all vastly different in style, but all were made with embroidery designs lovingly stitched by hand.

The church was overfilled, with people standing in the aisles and entrance foyer. Parts of the service were in English and some parts were in Norwegian. After the service, everyone lined up on the street outside the church to wait for the parade to begin.

She watched outside on the steps leading to the street, with her father, totally amazed by what she saw. There were a couple other women dressed in the same Telemark bunad as hers. Everyone at the event seemed very friendly. A few people even came up to her and commented on how beautiful her bunad was. Some people carried Norway's flag and others displayed banners from the local Norwegian groups. She made a mental note of a couple names—Daughters of Norway and Sons of Norway—so she could look them up online later and possibly join their groups to learn more about her heritage.

Standing in the hot sun, Sonja felt the strong rays of heat piercing through the heavy, one-hundred-percent wool, floor-length bunad. Needless to say, the costume was warm, especially since it was almost seventy degrees, which was an unusually high temp for mid-May. Moving to a shady spot, she observed people taking photos of the parade and the many women dressed in intriguing bunads walking along the street.

One younger man in particular, probably close to her age, appeared to be a professional photographer, and she couldn't help noticing he was extremely attractive. She was actually surprised to see so many people in their 20s and 30s at the event. She wasn't sure where the idea came from, but she had thought it would be almost all older people—her grandfather's age or at least her dad's age.

After the parade, a Nordic band played in the church's parking lot and a light lunch could be purchased. Lunch seemed more American than anything else to her, as it was hot dogs, chips, and pop. *But then, what do I really know about Norwegian traditions? Absolutely nothing.* She wasn't really sure what to expect, but she'd heard a lot about *lutefisk* being a Norwegian tradition.

"Having fun, Sonja?" her dad asked.

"I'm just trying to take it all in. It's actually a bit overwhelming." She continued observing the crowd.

Karl laughed. "You haven't seen anything yet. Just wait until you go to your first lutefisk dinner."

"Pardon me, but I'd love to take your picture, if you don't mind," said a voice from behind her.

She turned around. It was the good-looking photographer she'd noticed earlier. His blond hair framed a chiseled, clean-shaven face, and he stood tall, about six feet, his proud body trim and muscular. His deep blue eyes quickly scanned over her from head to toe, then lingered on her eyes.

"I'm Rolf Erickson. I'm taking pictures for *Viking* magazine." He continued staring at her.

Realizing she hadn't answered him, she said, "Sure."

After she posed so he could get a full shot, he took a few pictures. Then he checked the display screen on his camera to make sure he'd gotten some good ones.

He reached into his pocket, pulled out his business card, and handed it to her. "If you send me your email, I can forward the pictures to you."

"Thanks, my name is Sonja Thorson Miller." She took the card from him.

Her dad walked over and shook Rolf's hand. "I'm her father, Karl Miller."

"Nice to meet you, sir," Rolf said and turned toward Sonja. "A few of the women dressed in bunads are going over to the Lake Harriet Bandshell to pose for some more pictures. If you're free and interested, I'd love to have you join them."

"That'd be great. This is her first time wearing hers and it sounds like the perfect opportunity to be a part of the Syttende Mai celebration," Karl answered.

Rolf looked toward Sonja for her response.

"I'd love to. Thanks for asking." Her face lit up as she locked eyes with his.

"Great. We're meeting over there at two. See you then." Rolf smiled and walked away, snapping pictures as he went.

"Well, he certainly seemed like a nice young man." Karl grinned.

"It's only for a picture, Dad. Not a date," Sonja teased.

"For now. But he's interested in you," Karl said firmly.

"How would you know?" Sonja asked, trying to keep a straight face.

"A father can tell when a young buck is interested in his daughter. Trust me," Karl stated matter-of-factly.

"Whatever," Sonja quipped, hoping he was right then walked toward the vendor booths to see what treasures were being offered.

* * *

About one thirty, Sonja and her father pulled into the parking lot at the Lake Harriet Bandshell. Gazing out toward the water, she couldn't help but remember the many times she'd walked around this lake with her dad as a child. Located in the heart of Minneapolis, the beautiful lake was surrounded by a path that beckoned to joggers, walkers, bikers, and skaters. She would have to make a point of coming down here again for a nice, long walk around the lake.

There were about ten other ladies waiting, each dressed in a different bunad. She joined them just as Rolf approached.

"Thank you all for coming. I think we'll get some great shots here that will work well for the article I'm doing for *Viking* magazine. First, I will take single shots of everyone in various poses and then we'll do some group shots," Rolf instructed the group, but his eyes were glued on Sonja.

She was assigned to the end slot, probably because she was last to arrive. Her dad just smiled an I-told-you-so look from a distance. The women waited patiently and went up one by one to have their pictures taken. Since it was a large stage, he moved agilely around them, snapping pictures from different angles. Finally, it was her turn. She walked up the stairs to the stage. To say she wasn't a little nervous would've been a lie because she'd never done any type of modeling before and felt just a bit self-conscious about the whole thing.

"You're doing great. How about a big smile?" Rolf coaxed.

Sonja smiled, simply because she couldn't help it. His grin was contagious and dazzling, nothing like hers, she was sure.

"Now, how about you think about your first kiss?" Rolf suggested.

He snapped away furiously as she thought about that kiss. Her response was instantaneous and she didn't have a care in the world about how her face portrayed the memory.

"Sonja, you can stay up there, and let's have numbers eight and nine join her, please."

They came up and joined her on stage and he snapped away. Then the rest came up a couple at a time and soon everyone was on stage. They posed for many pictures before he was satisfied that he had enough shots.

"I can't thank you enough, ladies. Now, if you could all sign the release forms allowing me to use the pictures in the magazine and leave your email on the bottom of the paper so I can share the pictures with you, we'll be finished." Rolf gave everyone a form, his hand lingering on Sonja's as he passed her the last one.

She picked up the pen he'd offered and began filling it out. The others finished, handed Rolf their forms, and left. He came over to stand by her since she was the only one still there. When she was done, she looked up to catch him staring intently at her. He made her feel nervous but at the same time, her heart was beating madly in her chest.

She handed him the paper. "Thanks, it was fun. I'm excited to see the pictures."

"If you'd like, I would love to print some out for you. Maybe we could meet for coffee next week and I can bring some copies?"

"Sure," she said and couldn't help flashing him a big smile.

"Would the Starbucks at the Barnes and Noble in the Eden

Prairie Mall work for you?"

"That's perfect. I live in Eden Prairie," she responded.

"What night would be best for you?" he asked.

"How about Thursday at five thirty?" she suggested.

"Great. I'll send you an email this week to confirm." He watched as she looked over to where her dad was waiting patiently and watching them.

"I should go. My dad's waiting. See you Thursday." Her heart beat rapidly as she extended her hand, and a warm flush flowed through her body when they touched. Her hand lingered too long in his before she released it and walked away.

* * *

On Thursday, she sat at a café table in the Barnes and Noble store waiting for Rolf to arrive. Meeting men always filled her with dread, causing her to arrive early. Mainly because she was so nervous about being late, she ultimately ended up being fifteen minutes early. The email he'd sent yesterday was nice so there wasn't anything to worry about. She just hadn't gone out with anyone for months. No wonder she was jittery. She hated first dates, but heck, this wasn't even a date. Actually, she wasn't entirely sure what it was. Then, he walked through the door and his face immediately lit up when he saw her.

"So good to see you again, Sonja." His eyes roamed over her in a speculative evaluation. "You look really good. Without the bunad, I mean." He must have noticed the puzzled look on her face. "Never mind, that didn't come out right."

"That's okay. Thanks. I think? It was a compliment, wasn't it?"

"Absolutely! Sorry, it's just that sometimes it's hard to tell what a woman really looks like with those big bunads covering them from head to toe… I think I should just shut up now." He set his bag on the table and sat down.

"I understand what you're saying. It's fine." She was definitely glad she'd worn her skintight jeans and a fitted sweater to show off her figure.

"Can I get you something to drink?" he asked.

"Sure. But I'll come up with you so you don't have to try and remember my complicated coffee drink." She laughed and followed him to the counter.

After they ordered, they sat down once again. Rolf took out the photos and handed them to her. "I think your pictures turned out really great. You are extremely photogenic."

She picked up the pictures and looked at them one by one. There were ten in all. She wasn't so sure she agreed with the part about her being photogenic, but they were all very good shots. It probably had more to do with that he was a really good photographer.

Rolf watched her intently as she studied the pictures. When their names were called, he got up to get their drinks. He set them down as she finished studying the last picture. "What do you think?"

"They do look good. I think it's because you are a talented photographer. I don't usually like having my picture taken, but I do like these."

"You can keep them. I made these copies for you."

They both took sips of their drinks and didn't speak.

Rolf broke the silence. "I know this seems a little strange since we don't really know each other, so how about I go first? I grew up here in the Twin Cities, went to Chaska High School, and then Augsburg College. I have a degree in photojournalism. I freelance, work for *Viking m*agazine, as well as have my own photography company online where I sell my photos. I'm half Norwegian on my father's side and have been attending Norwegian events since I was a little kid. I'm single, haven't been in a serious relationship for over three years."

"Wow. I totally know you now! But probably, not really. Okay, here's my story. I'm from Eden Prairie, went to Eden Prairie High School, and then attended Mankato State University. My degree is in marketing and advertising, which I used to start my own company, SOMAR, where I do online marketing for small companies to get their names out in front of the public. The Syttende Mai parade was the first Norwegian event I've attended, even though I'm also half Norwegian. I'm single and have only dated casually because I haven't met anyone I liked enough to have a serious relationship with."

"I think I'm in love. Want to get married?" Rolf joked.

"Oh, definitely. It must be one of those 'love at first sight' situations."

They both laughed.

"Okay, I have a question. Why haven't you been to any Norwegian events?" Rolf asked.

"Unfortunately, my mother was the one who was one-hundred-percent Norwegian, but she died when I was very young. My dad took it extremely hard and since her parents were everything Norwegian, which reminded him of my mother, he cut off all ties with them. So, I was never able to learn about my heritage from them. Plus, they lived in Wisconsin so they weren't just down the street or anything like that," Sonja explained.

"I'm sorry you missed out on your Norwegian heritage growing up. It was a huge part of my life and put me where I am now. What made you finally reach out to come to the event?"

"My grandfather died recently and in his will instructed me to purchase a bunad from the Telemark area, where his parents were born, and to make plans to visit Norway. He left me the money to pay for all of it, of course. So, I ordered the bunad online and searched the internet to find local events where I could possibly wear it," Sonja answered, summarizing the stipulations of the will.

"Your grandfather must've been heartbroken that he wasn't able to share his ancestry with you. But what a wonderful legacy to leave you in his will. The financial means that would allow you to explore your heritage, even after he was gone," Rolf said, offering encouragement.

"In a heartfelt letter given to me by his lawyer, he expressed regret that he hadn't been able to share his pride and love for Norway with me since we lived so far apart. I never realized how much I missed, and probably how much he missed not being able to share it with me while he was still alive, until I attended his funeral last March," Sonja admitted, and her eyes became misty while she talked.

"So, do you know exactly where your relatives are over in Norway? Did he still have contact with them?"

"Of that, I'm not sure. My grandmother died shortly after my mother's death years ago, so I don't really have much to go on. I did receive a box of keepsakes from my grandparents' estate. I was planning on going through them and possibly taking a genealogy class to do more research," Sonja offered, and quickly brushed a tear away.

"The Mindekirken offers genealogy classes put on by the Norwegian Genealogy Association. I've wanted to take some of their classes for quite some time, to see how far back I can trace my family. I think they have one starting in June," Rolf offered.

"I would like to take that class, because if I'm going to Norway, it would be nice to know if I still have some relatives over there I could stop in to visit." Sonja smiled.

"I will check it out and email you the details," Rolf promised.

"Great! It would certainly be more fun to take a class with someone you know." Sonja's heart beat rapidly in her chest. Her attraction to Rolf was intense and the thought of getting to spend more time with him made her extremely happy.

"I've kept you talking for an hour now and you're probably starving. Let me buy you a sandwich. Then maybe we can continue our conversation for another hour?" Rolf asked, watching for her response.

"I haven't had dinner yet, so a sandwich would be great. And then we can see where the conversation leads," she said, as she smiled across the table at him.

* * *

Rolf called her the next day to let her know where to register for the genealogy class. Signup was available on the Mindekirken's website.

Unfortunately, the following week, he needed to be in Moorhead for a photo shoot of the Hjemkomst Viking Ship and a Viking re-enactment festival, instead of spending more time with Sonja. While he was gone, though, he called her almost every night, and she found herself looking forward to the next time he would call.

On Saturday, she woke to a bright, sunny day with temps expected in the seventies. It would be a great day for a walk and to be outdoors, so she headed to Lake Harriet.

She paced herself so she could make it the whole way around the lake. When she finished, she sat down on a bench to rest and look out over the water. The lake was still cold from winter, but would be warming up a little more each day. Soon the beach would be full of people in their swimsuits, enjoying sunbathing and swimming. The gentle sound of waves rolling onto the beach filled the air.

It was a vastly different day from the cold and dreary day of her grandfather's funeral in March, only a few months ago. The memory was vivid in her mind as she recalled the day.

Sitting in a pew at the front of the church, she'd reached into her purse to pull out another Kleenex to wipe the tears from her face. Tears that, of their own accord, continued to roll down her cheeks. Her dad, an insurance salesman from a stout German heritage, sat quietly beside her.

Ole Thorson, her grandfather, lay in a coffin at the front of the church while the pastor told wonderful stories about his life. A life she had not been a part of. Her mother, Greta Thorson Miller, had died in an accident twenty years ago when her car was struck broadside by a drunk driver. Miraculously, the drunk driver survived. Unfortunately, her mother hadn't. She'd only been five years old at the time, so she remembered very little about her mother or her mother's family.

She'd listened intently to the stories about her grandfather's life, realizing it was most likely her last chance to get to know anything about him. After her mother had died, she and her dad only went to visit her grandparents a few times because each time they'd visited, her father became extremely depressed knowing that the city of Stoughton was where the love of his live had grown up. He'd felt so much anger since his wife was no longer alive, but the drunk driver was still living and able to go on with his life.

Listening to the stories told by the pastor and other friends of Ole Thorson, she'd realized her grandfather had been a very likable person. Someone she would probably have enjoyed spending time with. But with her mother gone, the connection had been broken. She felt as if her heart had shattered into a million pieces while the last remnants of her mother slipped away.

Two of the hymns were sung in Norwegian at the First Lutheran Church in Stoughton, Wisconsin, and after the service, everyone had followed the coffin to the cemetery next door.

Time seemed to stand still, but then she'd found herself walking slowly back to the church and descending the steps to the basement. Members of the church had set out photo boards filled with pictures of Ole and her grandmother, Gunhild. She'd taken pictures of each board, then went back to intently look at each picture board to take in as much as she could about her mother's life in the small city.

Shortly after she'd memorized the last picture, she'd snuck outside and strolled slowly toward the cemetery to her grandfather's grave.

She'd felt so empty inside and her heart was broken. Besides her father, who refused to talk about her mother or her mother's family, Ole Thorson, a complete stranger to her, was the only other person who'd ever really known her mother.

She'd felt the tears forming in her eyes once again and voluntarily let them roll furiously down her cheeks. Those tears weren't for her mother or her grandfather. No, they were for her and all the memories she'd missed out on during her young life.

But today was a sunny day and so was her future outlook on life. She was pursuing her Norwegian heritage along with a hot Norwegian guy who made her feel wonderful with just the touch of his hand. A smile crossed her face as she got up to walk around the lake one more time.

*　*　*

Two weeks later, Sonja walked into the Mindekirken's basement for the genealogy class where she was meeting Rolf. They hadn't gotten together since their Starbucks sort-of date, but had emailed multiple times a day and talked on the phone. He sent her links to interesting Norwegian articles he'd come across, which led to her frantically searching the internet to find things she could share.

That first day of class, she sat down next to Rolf, who'd saved her a chair at his table. She was ecstatic to learn how to research her genealogy, and listened intently as the instructor gave the info they all would need to get started. She opened her laptop and began getting set up with a login for the genealogy site.

The class went on for four weeks and she looked forward to each one, as with each week she came closer to finding her relatives in Norway. After each class, Sonja and Rolf would go grab a bite to eat and talk more about themselves and their dreams. And as each week went on, her feelings for Rolf grew stronger. After the last class, they went to Matt's Bar to celebrate with their famous burgers.

"Have you had any luck contacting some of the names you've found in the Telemark area?" Rolf asked, while they waited for their burgers and fries.

"Just got one today from a cousin of my mother's. It was from one of their kids who is my age, Anna Lise, and she would love to meet a relative from America," Sonja proudly announced.

"That's wonderful. Are you planning on going to Norway this summer?" Rolf asked, as the waitress brought their beers.

"I would like to, but I don't really want to go alone. I have a cousin, Marie, who lives in Texas and another cousin, Ingrid, who lives in Seattle. They were also in grandfather's will with the same stipulation to spend the money to purchase a bunad and travel to Telemark, Norway. Unfortunately, I'm not so sure I want to go with them. I've never spent any time with them and really don't know them at all," Sonja confessed.

"I can understand that. Traveling with people can be difficult and if you don't really know them, it can be even worse. What about your dad? Would he go?" Rolf asked.

"I haven't asked him. Remember, he never wanted anything to do with the Norwegian stuff. So, I don't think he'd go." She'd thought about asking him but hadn't done it.

"You might want to check out Brekke Tours. They have multiple travel packages to Norway and then you would go with a group. You could always add on days to go on your own to visit your relatives." Rolf watched the conflicting emotions cross her face.

"That would probably be the best thing to do. I could check out their packages to find out the best one and then at least ask my cousins if they'd like to go."

After enjoying their burgers, Rolf walked Sonja to her car.

"Sonja, I like spending time with you. I know we've both been busy with our jobs lately, but I was thinking maybe we could go out this weekend. I heard about a new restaurant, Valhalla, near Stillwater that I'd love to take you to for dinner Saturday night."

She stared at Rolf. A guy she couldn't find anything about not to like, and who actually appeared slightly nervous while he waited for an answer. He made her feel so at ease and she loved the bond they'd formed searching the archives of Norway for distant relatives, along with the emails and phone calls they'd shared. Nothing would make her happier than to spend more time with him because she knew Rolf was a guy she could easily fall for. She could only hope he felt the same.

"I'd like that. It sounds like a fun place," Sonja answered.

"Great! I'll call you tomorrow," he said.

And then, he leaned down and kissed her—first, a light kiss on the lips, which deepened and left her yearning for more. Sonja was sure she was in Valhalla at that very moment. But it was over way too quickly and she definitely wanted more. She could tell he was holding back and trying to be a gentleman, as he leaned away a little to gauge her reaction. Her eyes were filled with passion and she didn't try to hide it, but more of Valhalla was best left for another time. Besides, a parking lot was not the place she wanted to pursue this fire burning between them and find out where it would lead. To his surprise and hers, she leaned into him and boldly kissed him, then backed away.

"I'd better get going. Talk to you tomorrow," she said, and got into her car quickly before she changed her mind.

* * *

Sonja spent the next day searching the internet for package trips to Norway. She found Brekke Travel did have the best prices. In fact, they had a package that would work perfectly. She emailed the info to her cousins, along with her preferred dates of travel. At the last minute, she decided to send it to her dad, as well. Although, she had no hopes that any of them would take her up on the offer to accompany her on the trip.

Before she knew, it was Saturday and she was dressing for her date with Rolf. Unsure what to wear, she stared into her closet. She finally picked a recently purchased t-shirt, printed with a replica of the Norwegian flag, and a pair of skintight blue jeans to accentuate her trim body. He was picking her up soon so she quickly finished curling her hair and putting on her makeup.

She was excited to check out this new restaurant with a Norwegian theme. As they walked in, she observed the various different Viking shields adorning the walls and a table holding three Viking helmets with horns, placed on furs.

"Wow, this is really cool," she commented, as they took their seats at the table.

They looked the menu over and made their choices for the waiter.

She ordered the meatballs and he ordered the cod basket, along with Valhalla's own home-brewed Viking ale.

"I have to say, I'm impressed with this place," Rolf said, as they were leaving. "How is your trip planning going?"

"I'll send you the details for the Brekke package I picked. But, it looks like I will have to travel alone if I go. My cousins finally got back to me and said they weren't sure they could take time off from work this summer. "

"What about your dad? Did you ask him to go?"

"I sent him the info, but I didn't get a response yet." Sonja stopped walking when they reached his car and he opened the door for her to get in.

During the whole ride home, she was anticipating whether she would get another kiss. And, when he walked her up to the door, he took her in his arms, and kissed her long and hard, leaving her breathless. She knew she wanted him but she wasn't sure how much further she wanted to go at this point. After a couple more long, sensual kisses, he said goodnight and left.   He hadn't pushed her and it was obvious he was taking his time, which was perfectly fine with her. But the other question she kept asking herself was if she should ask him to accompany her on the trip to Norway.

* * *

Four weeks later, Sonja finished packing her suitcases for her two-week trip to Norway. Alone. No one had been able to go with her, so she decided to go anyway. She'd never gotten up the courage to ask Rolf, even though their relationship had been moving along in the right direction. It just seemed a little odd to go on a trip with someone you'd only recently met and weren't sleeping with yet. Even though she knew they would get to that point soon.

Her dad was picking her up shortly to take her to the airport.

Sonja just finished lining her bags up at the door when he arrived.

"I think it takes great courage to go on an international trip alone. But no one should go alone, especially a young woman such as yourself," he said, as he loaded her bags into the car.

"Dad...we talked about this and no one could go," Sonja replied.

"Well, not exactly. I decided your mother would never forgive me if I let you go by yourself, so I'm going with you," he announced.

"I can't believe you didn't tell me before now." A huge smile spread across her face.

"I wasn't sure if I could get away, and then I wasn't sure I could get a ticket and still get on the tour until last week," Karl explained.

"Thank you, Daddy. I can't tell you how happy this makes me," she said, and hugged him before getting into the car.

Minutes later, they arrived at the airport and made their way to the ticket counter for Icelandic Air located at the Minneapolis St. Paul Humphrey Terminal.

She couldn't believe her eyes. There in the corridor was Rolf, with a suitcase, walking toward her.

"Rolf, what are you doing here?" Her heart was pounding so hard in her chest and she felt lightheaded. Was she really going to be able to share this trip to Norway with him?

"Well, you know my relatives are in the Telemark area, too. But the main reason is, I wanted to experience this with you." He released the handle of his roller bag and set his backpack down on the floor.

Sonja let go of her bag, set her purse down, and closed the distance between them. She wrapped her arms around his neck and kissed him like she never wanted to let him go. This was going to be the trip of a lifetime, and she couldn't wait to spend it with the two most important men in her life.

Rolf held Sonja tightly in his arms, returning her kisses, then he leaned back to look into her dazzling eyes. "My favorite saying is, 'This is the first day of the rest of your life,' and I'd like to make it the first day of the rest of our lives together."

Tears formed in Sonja's eyes. "I'd like that, too."

They heard someone coughing behind them. "May be a good thing I'm coming along to chaperone the four of you."

"Four?" Sonja asked.

"Yes, your cousins, Ingrid and Marie, are meeting us in Oslo. They couldn't come for the whole time so they will be meeting up with us for the second week."

Sonja couldn't help the huge smile spreading across her face. She was positive this was the best day of her life, so far anyway. She was also sure her grandfather never expected his last will and testament would bring them all together. Not to mention, help her find Rolf, who she was extremely positive would end up being a permanent part of her life.

This could very well end up being her very own *Nor-Way to Love!*

ABOUT THE AUTHOR

Rose Marie Meuwissen, a first-generation Norwegian American born and raised in Minnesota, always tries to incorporate her Norwegian heritage into her writing. After receiving a BA in Marketing from Concordia University, a Masters in Creative Writing from Hamline University soon followed. Minnesota is still where she calls home.

She has been a member of Romance Writers of America (RWA) since 1995 and has attended multiple RWA National Conferences and Romantic Times Conventions. In 2012, she became co-founder of Romancing the Lakes of Minnesota Writers, a local RWA Chapter in Minnesota.

She has traveled around the world, including Scandinavia, but still has many places to see, enjoys attending Scandinavian events, writing conferences and is usually busy writing Contemporary and Viking Time Travel Romances, Motorcycle Rally Screenplays, Nordic Cozy Murder Mysteries, WWII Nazi Occupation of Norway Historical fiction and Norwegian Traditions Children's Books.

Visit her at:
www.rosemariemeuwissen.com
www.realnorwegianseatlutefisk.com
www.romancingtherose.blogspot.com

Taking Chances—a contemporary romance novel set in Minnesota and Arizona.

Blizzard of Love—a short romance story set in Lutsen, Minnesota on Lake Superior, available in the anthology, *Romancing the Lakes of Minnesota—Winter.*

Railroad Ties—a short romance story set in Two Harbors,

Minnesota on Lake Superior, available in the anthology, *Romancing the Lakes of Minnesota—Autumn*.

Hot Summer Nights—a short romance story set on Prior Lake, available in the anthology, *Romancing the Lakes of Minnesota—Summer*.

Dancing in the Moonlight—a short romance story set on Mille Lacs Lake, available in the anthology, *Love in the Land of Lakes*.

Real Norwegians Eat Lutefisk—a Children's book about the tradition of Lutefisk presented in both English and Norwegian.

Real Norwegians Eat Rømmegrøt—The second Children's book in the series about the tradition of Rømmegrøt presented in both English and Norwegian.

ROMANCE IN SPACE AND TIME
Ingrid Anderson Sampo

Lake Minnetonka - Wayzata, MN

It all began with a bit of research and a class I taught. I never dreamed it would lead me across continents and time to a poet years my senior who had captured my heart. Maybe I should have. After all, he was considered a romantic—a Romantic poet, that is.

I had a brief encounter with his writing in Senior Literature, accompanied by a high school infatuation of great proportions. This deepened into a budding relationship when I embarked on an English major in my undergraduate college years and during my Romantic Literature course. I fell in love with the Romantic poets, especially Percy Bysshe Shelley.

Little did I know, it would draw me into a master's, then later a doctorate and the coveted post at the University of St. Catherine in St. Paul, Minnesota. It was during my fourth year at St. Catherine's that I launched my research preceding the writing of an in-depth book on Shelley—unearthing information heretofore unknown about the sensitive writer and complex man. Three months into the research, I experienced feelings similar to my first crush in high school, burgeoning into my soulful college passion.

Realizing I needed to make sense of my emotions for a nineteenth century Romantic poet, I scheduled a type of "therapy session." Before I knew it, I had texted Janelle, a fellow college professor and friend, to meet me at Starbucks for my "therapy."

As we sat over steaming lattes, she stared at me in disbelief. "You are infatuated with a poet who was buried in the 1820s?"

Smiling with a suggestion of a chuckle, I avoided eye contact. Peering out the window at the flowering apple trees in all their spring glory ringing Lake Minnetonka, I jumped in, "It's love, not merely an infatuation. You see, I know his deepest thoughts—all expressed in the poetry I've been reading and sharing for years. And he just happens to be unbelievably handsome. I've seen artists' renderings of him. In fact, he's exactly my age. At least, he was twenty-six back in 1818."

"Angelica, this is a no-win for you. I'm worried about you. More than worried. I'm *afraid* for you. I don't want you to waste your best years chasing after an impossible dream and a fictitious romance."

"I know our relationship is impossible, but the more I research him and his writing, the more I love him and his soul. I can't remember being so happy."

"You should be dating some professor—one of your colleagues. Let me introduce you to Duncan. He's new at the University of St. Thomas, your brother school. I'll throw a dinner party for, say, half a dozen of our friends, so it won't be an obvious set-up. Please?"

"Well, maybe later. Right now, I must remain focused on the research for my book. I'm on a deadline with my editor." Frustrated, I threw up my hands. I'm sure my face was contorted with stress.

"Your book about Percy Shelley," Janelle said with a knowing look. Sarcasm shaded her voice.

"Well, yes."

With an eye roll and a shrug, Janelle said, "I give up. I hope all goes well with your book and your infatuation."

* * *

Janelle was a true friend, despite my shucking off her advice. She was my go-to person with the joys I celebrated and the disappointments I mourned. In our talks, she consistently revealed discernment and wisdom. Not surprising, as she taught psychology at St. Catherine's.

We were hired the same year and found much in common, with the exception of our experience with men.

Janelle was living with a man I knew she would marry. She had a knack for understanding men. Her relationship with Steve was smooth sailing, not even a ripple in the waters of their love for one another.

I couldn't forget her talk of Steve. "He's everything I've ever wanted in a man—sense of humor, bent toward the spiritual, intelligent but not stuffy. And he adores me."

"He sounds too good to be true," I commented with envy. I remembered that remark when she and I talked of my infatuation with Percy and she accused me of inventing a man without a flaw.

Janelle knew I rarely dated. My class load was heavy with five preparations. I taught everything from Romantic poets to 19th Century British novelists. That semester, I had designed and launched a class on the Bronte sisters and their contributions to British literature.

Janelle's comments had drawn me into a bit of self-analysis. If I were perfectly honest with myself, I could say I was escaping real life relationships with this growing passion for Percy Shelley. As my mother would say, I was a "late bloomer." My first date was to the Senior Prom with a boy who could have won over me in a competition for most profoundly shy.

In college, I dated sporadically, blaming the crowd I ran with—men and women who seemed to be forever locked into a hanging-out mode, never dating seriously for any length of time.

As an English major, I was caught up in an amazing amount of reading and in the worlds of the characters I read, analyzed, and wrote about. My closest friends told me I lived vicariously through these characters to the point of crushing on some of the male gender.

I have to admit their observations were spot on. I guess you could say I had a social disability, at least when it came to men.

* * *

One day, deep into my research, I knew a profound desire I could not quench—a need to journal about my feelings for Percy. After a moment, I realized I was composing a love letter to the poet.

Longing for greater closeness to Percy, and recognizing a gap in in my research, I convinced myself only a trip to Florence could fill my empty places. I recalled Percy had lived in Florence, Italy, for some years—a prolific time for his writing. Given my questionable reasoning, I was airborne in two days. Within three, I was standing outside a near replica of Percy Shelley's one-time Florence home, built on the same plot where the original residence, destroyed by fire, had once stood. On a whim, I placed my journal entry, aka love letter to Percy, in the mailbox affixed to the building.

Checking Percy's parcel post box at his residence the next day, I discovered the letter was gone, and so I posted another. By day four, I extricated a letter from deep within the box that was written to me and bore the address of the one-time Shelley residence. The formal script evoked that of his time.

The envelope's contents, an essay on love entitled, "Hymn to the Intellectual," sent my heart hammering within my chest. Leaning against the mailbox, somehow I regained a semblance of equilibrium. Still gasping, I struggled for breath.

"*Signora*, are you well?"

"Yes, fine, thank you." I lied to the kindly older, yet handsome Italian who'd grabbed my elbows and righted me.

* * *

That night poring over my research notes, I sensed a presence within my hotel room. A tap on my shoulder was unmistakable. A voice in my head was quiet, yet clear, not unlike a thought. "Our connection is real. I feel it, too. I knew at once when I received your letters. Come to me. You can do this. You traveled to Florence. You can journey into the 1800s."

"How?" I cried in exasperation. Again, came the touch that calmed my fears and exhilarated my senses.

As I reached across my worktable for Percy's essay on love, I was blinded, perceiving only blackness as I tunneled through space at a terrifying, warp speed. Shaken, I landed inside Percy's Florence residence with oil-burning lamps and candles illuminating the entrance. I could see him through the door to a nearby room.

It had happened. Shocked and fearful, all I could think was—what am I to do? I calmed myself as best I could. And then, like a typical researcher and teacher, I decided to conduct an interview, despite the fact I was in my night clothes. I had changed for bed before my travels. After my initial embarrassment, I realized a nightie was closest in style to clothes of the time—a serendipitous occurrence.

The reception area was appointed with a burnished-gold chandelier, adding cheeriness to a room of stark gray-green walls and cornices. I was greeted by a courteous but austere house servant. "What is your business here?"

"I am here at the invitation of Mr. Shelley."

Looking doubtful, the servant beckoned me into the room where Percy sat at a desk, ensconced by stacks of papers. Plumed stylus in hand, Percy was penning something by the light of an oil lamp. I had stepped closer to view the page, filled with short lines indicative of poetry.

"You wished to meet with me?" He spoke in a resonant voice that was reserved in tone.

I knew he had not yet recognized me. And so, I explained I wanted to learn more about his writing. We were awkward at first, relating as interviewer and interviewee. I asked him about the details of his works that puzzled me. Patiently, he answered each question.

"In your poem, 'Ozymandius,' was Ozymandius really Ramses of Egypt as some say?"

"Actually, yes."

"I can see the meaning many assigned it. But please, I'd like to hear the explanation in your own words."

Succinctly, yet deeply, he shared his thoughts.

Our eyes locked and held as if we looked into each other's souls. At that point, I was certain he knew I was the person who left a love note and traveled to him across time at his urging.

"Though we have had but brief moments together, I feel as if I have known you for years. Our connection transcends time and the centuries that separate us," Percy said, a look of wonder painted across his face.

Our link was intellectual as well as emotional. We both

recognized this and so he, honoring our intellectual connection, said to me, "You have more questions about my writing?"

"Oh, yes." And so I plumbed the depths of his mind. I queried him about "Hymn to the Intellectual Beauty," asking for greater understanding of his work.

"Intellect is non-material. Thus intellectual beauty is an unseen power beyond the reach of the senses. Rather, it accounts for awareness that occasionally arises. It offers grace and truth to the natural world and to a moral consciousness. This remains a mystery regardless of religion and philosophy and is beyond human knowledge."

We talked of his thoughts on religion, expressed in works like his "Necessity of Atheism," with which I disagreed. We could discuss it without argument, and I distinctly had the sense he was considering my view. Conversely, his written thoughts urging the right for women to vote we both passionately embraced and discussed at length.

"Now I understand your talk of others' views of my writing. That is of course in the future, is it not?"

"Yes. You became a highly lauded and regarded poet."

He was amazed. "Truly? Things need to change dramatically then. I have but few followers now, mostly my close friends."

This conversation, this time together was my dream—a passion based in the written word, in the mind, and in the soul. I marveled at his mind—at once deeply intellectual and simultaneously passionate, and I said as much.

Looking into his soulful dark eyes, I imagined I could see my reflection—so linked were we in spirit and soul. He traced my face with his fingers. Brushed my cheek with his lips. Kissed me on the mouth with great emotion. My life in the past versus the present became unimportant. A magnetic pull drew us together. Soon we were kissing again and again—our mouths seeking one another, our bodies drawn to each other, removing all semblance of space between us. I became unconscious of time—until the sun's rays broke into the room the next morn.

Hours turned into days, and days, weeks. We talked, wrote, ate, loved, slept, and then the cycle would repeat.

As we visited the city's highest point, I took in the beauty that was Florence. Exuberant with the joy of the moment, I greeted a family who were just steps away, also enjoying the view. "Lovely, isn't it?"

There was no response. At first, I thought they did not understand English. On further reflection, I realized they did not hear nor see me. It was then I became aware, only to Percy and those within his home had I been physically seen in 1818. To all others, I was invisible.

At the beginning of week two, we left his residence for the cathedral that Florentines lovingly called *the* Duomo—undeniably one of the finest cathedrals in Europe. A magnificently crafted gold door welcomed us, drawing us into the cathedral's ethereal beauty and its mystical spirituality.

We entered into the holy hush of the room alight with candles. Arms around each other, we then dropped them to our sides. Percy said our physical intimacy did not seem appropriate in such a place. An avowed atheist, Percy appeared to be struck by the holiness of the Duomo. In fact, he turned to me and said, searchingly, "Perhaps I was a bit premature in determining my spiritual focus. In here, there is something more."

Percy was the true romantic—surprising me with gifts of jewelry and flowers, serenading me below our window. Lovemaking was never rushed and always passionate and satisfying.

"I have never been so happy," Percy effused. Mentioning his essay "On Love," he said, "How could I have known of this mystery before I met you? Our minds and spirits are joined. Our hearts beat in perfect time with one another."

As he gazed penetratingly into my eyes, he said with passion and tenderness, "If I wrote a novel, you would be the protagonist. If poetry or an essay, it would be about my love for you. If a play, you would be the leading lady. And always, you would be as you are right here before me—witty, intelligent, sensual, and too beautiful for words. And thus, I would labor long into the night watches to find the exact words to describe you."

We sat over *vino* at a charming sidewalk café and basked in the sun only Florence could provide. Fresh, clean with the promise of a day to remember. And that it was—strolling along the lovely Arno River and boarding a rowboat.

Percy, in a manly state of mind and heart, insisted on rowing, even though he was quick to add that I was an equal and had every right and ability to take on the task of guiding the boat.

When I laughed delightedly, he queried, "Are you making fun of me?"

"Dearest, never. It is just that I am so happy and you make me so. And, once again, I see what is perhaps the most attractive of your many attributes—you are truly fair-minded. You see me as an equal. Do you know how empowering and exciting that is?"

Before I knew what was happening, he moved toward me, dropping the oars into the water, kissing my face, my neck, my shoulders, and pulling me down into the boat.

The only problem was that when we came up for air from our romantic encounter, we were stranded without oars. Drifting down the Arno, we called for help.

Finally, another boat, considerably larger than ours, came into view. In our excitement, we nearly upended our vessel.

Following our rescue, we could not stop laughing. Whenever we recalled the boat trip, the comedy of that moment emerged once again and birthed more laughter. When we were around others, they were inevitably confused, unable to fathom how mention of a leisurely boat trip could inspire such jocularity. We kept private the details and the cause of our misadventure.

* * *

Percy was invited to attend an event in his honor, given by his friends as he was not yet received as a poet worthy of acclaim. He begged me to accompany him. "My love, I cannot bear for us to be apart. I would be truly honored if you would deign to be my guest. You would draw the attention of every male in the room with your soulful presence and exquisite beauty. And in conversation, you would transfix their minds and souls with your intelligence and sensitivity."

"Will I not be invisible to them?"

"I don't think you will. Remember the other day when my friend Emil visited? I introduced you to him. I am certain my friends see you. Or else you are becoming more a part of nineteenth century Florence."

"How can I refuse?"

I donned a gown from Percy's closet—one of green velvet with a crinoline and a deep sweetheart neckline, emphasizing my green eyes. I never felt more beautiful, from within and without—Percy's doing.

As we entered the home of poet Lord Byron, cut-glass crystal chandeliers streamed light and prism-like shadows. It was exhilarating to talk with the famous Lord Byron. He was a flirt. I noticed Percy moved closer whenever the Lord spoke with me.

Interestingly, as we danced and talked with his friends, I discovered I truly was visible. I was existing, at least to Percy's friends, in 1818. Was this a sign that I had made the transition? For a moment, I knew panic and joy simultaneously. Could I be forever embedded in the 1800s? Yet, I would be with the man I loved. And the joy of the moment overtook me. We danced across the parquet floors amidst beautiful people costumed in silks, laces, and velvets the hues of royal purple, passion pink, and deep claret. I felt as if I were in a movie from another era.

Many parties followed. Elegant. Enchanting. Stimulating within the framework of our literary discussions and given the presence of Lord Byron and many aspiring poets and writers.

One ball lingered in my memory more than the others. Thoughtful and imaginative, Percy planned it all. After learning it was my birthday, he threw a party on the grandest scale. He adapted standard parlor games of the time into comical mind-benders, more humorous to me given the time lapse involved.

With a look of exuberance and a gesture as grand as his arms could reach, Percy launched one of the best of the games—What if…?

"What if you woke one morning and wanted more than anything to be with those damn Yankees in America, and you lifted your arms, willing it. With one blink of the eye, you were flying over the Atlantic. Within half a candle burn, you were there, shaking the hand of the President of the United States of America."

"But that is too incredible," Lord Byron bellowed. "There must be a means of transport—a buggy with wings." The glint in his eyes gave him away.

Guests laughed uproariously and that was the beginning of many brain-children—all ridiculous and laugh-out-loud funny. Unless you were from a far-off century and could see the possibilities of transforming ludicrous ideas into inventions commonly used in the future.

Percy shared the *pièce de résistance*. "What if you could will yourself to travel in time to the ancient days of Rome or into the future—say the year 2016?"

A hush fell over the group. With a perceptive look, one woman said, "You talk as if from experience."

Percy made the save with another surprise he pulled out of his trove of crazy schemes. Each guest chose a favorite poem or story, pantomiming it for us, the audience, to guess.

Entertainment was building into reconstructed renderings of literature, transplanting a dialogue, scene, or character from one work into another. Most were guessed quickly by this group of literati.

The silliest was created by a less than learned guest who latched onto an easy Shakespearean recall, taken from *Romeo and Juliet*, and inserted it into *Macbeth*, yet another Shakespearean play. The guest placed Juliet's line, 'Romeo, Romeo, wherefore art thou Romeo?' into the mouth of Lady Macbeth.

Partying and dancing far into the night, we often changed partners mid-dance. Every hour on the hour there was a birthday serenade just for me—one via a string quartet and another soloed by a visiting operatic soprano, and later, a piano concerto rendering numerous glissandos.

Near the close of the party, I thought, *this is what life would be like if I remained.* I wanted nothing more. I did for a few days, that is.

The longer the time I spent with Percy, the more I could not imagine life without him. But what could be done? I must give up either my 21st century life in academia or life in 1818 with Percy.

Part and parcel of my entire being was my professorship and the stimulating academic world of study, research, and the exchange of ideas. Teaching classes. Leading symposiums. Writing about the literary mysteries of meaning and interpretation that I and other researchers investigated and resolved.

Perhaps my first love was the exhilaration of guiding promising St. Catherine students into the world of great literature. Some to create their own. Others to delve into the deep and timeless messages of that literature.

In spite of interacting with Percy's friends—soon-to-be prominent literary figures of that time—I had left behind the literary world I knew. A world that filled my head with knowledge, offered sustenance to my soul, yet all but ignored my heart. I finally said as much to Percy.

Initially, he only heard talk of lack in my life, especially lack of love. "I can see a faint hope for me. Within you, there is a birth of a desire to stay." Percy grasped my hands, kissing them gently. Turning my palms upward, he covered them with sensuous kisses.

I was not about to surrender. "What if you came with me into the 21st century? It must be possible. If I could travel back in time, you could travel forward. Just think of the honors you would receive, for in the future your work would be deemed to have merit. You would experience acclaim for your literary gift and your perception of life. People would clamor to hear you reading your works and explaining their meaning. Your launch into the 21st century would be nothing short of a sensation, capturing the world's attention."

"Yes, my dear, but you are determined that I surrender my current life and you keep yours. Is that fair?"

Percy rose from his chair, began to pace, and with every step, his voice grew in intensity. He was like an English barrister intent on proving the defendant's guilt in a court of law.

His words backed me into the dead end of my impossible decision. His arguments encroached on my space, diminishing by the moment. I once had options. Now that was not so clear.

"How can you pressure me so?" He continued pacing. "To use my desire and love for you as a weapon to force your way?"

"Percy, how can you say that? You seek to control me." In one moment, I was fearful of losing him and then in the next, I was filled with wrath at his lack of fairness that I had credited him with in the past.

His voice rose to a shout. "I have for these past weeks been available for whatever you needed or desired. Now you say I give you no choice? You are giving me no choice."

I ran from the room, seeking refuge in the far reaches of the house. Percy did not follow. He left me to regret my words, feel the anguish of rejection, and fear that our love had been destroyed. That night we slept in separate rooms.

In the morning, I was awakened to breakfast in bed, served by Percy—at once penitent and amorous. "We need to talk of this, not argue. I attacked you and your rights to be a confident woman who determines her own destiny. Please, forgive me."

"Oh, my love, I am so relieved. You give me new hope. I am sorry I reacted in anger."

His eyes said even more than his words as he drew me to him. Soon, my partially eaten breakfast was set aside.

Our love did not solve our dilemma. It was not only a matter of who was to concede what life. It was also a matter of leaving behind close relationships in each of our lives. My work colleagues, my mother, who just happened to be my best friend and recently widowed. My devoted friend Janelle who had seen me through my joys and sorrows. How could I turn away from her? She who was always there for me.

And then, there were Percy's close friends and fellow writers. Perhaps, even more importantly, the matter of his wife, away all these weeks—a telling reality. I had discovered her existence the end of the first week of my stay. I asked Percy about the identity of a woman in an artist's rendering, adorning the sitting room wall.

"How could you not have told me? I am not in the habit of cheating with another woman's husband." But he assured me their relationship was over long before I had appeared.

Moments later, after the shock wore off, I remembered my research. Of course he had a wife during this time period. I had been so infatuated, I had not been thinking clearly. My memory had become fuzzy.

Despite his assurances concerning the end of his relationship with his wife, my writer's intuition told me there was still an attachment. Just days after our argument, a letter arrived from her. It was a lightning bolt striking Percy's plans for a future with me. I knew the letter was of great import. His silence spoke to me more than any words. He remained secluded the better part of the day, only to appear for dinner and inform me that after our meal, we must talk alone, away from prying servants.

His words struck me with the force of a bullet. "My wife is with child."

Attempting to recover from the shock, I said, "I'm sorry to have to say this, but are you sure it is yours? After all, she's been away for some time."

"Only three months. She's lived in a secluded area with maiden aunts. My feelings for her dwindled to a mere ember and grew cold. Returning to her is impossible. You and I have discovered the fullness of love. Yet, I cannot comprehend leaving this time and place, destroying any opportunity to welcome my child into the world and guide him through his childhood years. Granted, it would be as a divorced man, and thus I would see him rarely. Still, can't you see why I must stay?"

"What of my many relationships that I have left behind? What of my budding career? Are these non-issues?" I picked up the nearest book, slamming it to the floor and exiting the room.

I'm not certain which launched me into my trajectory—my anger or the epiphany of our impossible situation. My spirits traveled on a journey from anger to despair. I was in a vacuum with no means of support. Deprived of energy, I was weaving.

As strength drained from me, I thought, this must be how it feels to die. Just as I had entered Percy's world, I departed, passing at warp speed through a darkened, narrow tunnel. On this, my second trip through time and space, I should have been calm. After all, I had experienced the journey before, had survived and thrived. I had learned, though, that entering another century was not without its problems.

However, this time I was terrified of leaving Percy. Frightened about what he might do or what might happen to him if he followed me. Fearful of my return from the distant past. Would that mean I had aged and would be close to death? My pores rained sweat. My throat was as dry as the reeds in Percy's dining table arrangement. I was certain my heart had entered its own journey bound for fibrillation. And yet, there I was back in my Florence hotel room in the early morning hours. My head in my hands, I had fallen asleep over my research and writing. Devastated, I cried myself to sleep.

When I woke at noon, I realized I had been given a wondrous gift. Not only had I met and loved the man of my dreams, I knew the answers to my perplexing questions about his writing, his thoughts, his very self. For better or for worse, I had a most personal time with the poet. An interview of all interviews. He was at once mindful and intimate. In explaining the meaning of his writing, he even quoted literary minds of his time who had echoed his thoughts. He closed all the gaps in my research and my desires. I wrote voraciously, making certain I had on paper all he had shared with me.

* * *

My writing completed and publisher's deadline met, I once again was sitting over lattes with Janelle at the Lake Minnetonka Starbucks. Early summer had retained its spring green freshness.

I told her everything and she almost believed me. However, she did say, "You know, you woke up head in hands over your writing. You could have dreamed it all.

"Either way, you have some amazing information to share in your writing. I'm sure it will be honored with an award."

I could not hold myself back from saying, "That is because I received the material first-hand from Percy."

Her prediction about an award was prophetic. Just five months following the publishing of the book, I received a phone call. The affected and slightly pompous voice was cordial. It seemed fitting for the representative of the Minnesota Book Awards.

"I am calling to inform you of an honor you are to receive in the form of an awards presentation. This Minnesota Book Award for Scholarly Nonfiction is being given to you for unsurpassed research and insight concerning a Romantic poet."

Despite the satisfaction of publishing a work of quality research and the excitement of being honored with an award, I was deeply saddened over the loss of Percy. At one point, I thought if I called out to him while reading his writing, possibly I could attempt to reunite our souls. Perhaps I could return to him. Or he could travel into present time and space. But nothing. No dream, no vision, no travel, no appearance. I was devastated, stripped of hope.

At the awards dinner, I sat with Janelle. Approaching our table was a man who from a distance looked vaguely familiar. Janelle whispered to me that this was the man she'd wanted me to meet, the new professor of English poetry at the University of St. Thomas.

Janelle motioned him over to our table. "I want you to meet Duncan Bysshe. And, Duncan, this is our honored guest tonight, Angelica Champeau."

Turning to me and taking my hand, he congratulated me and complimented my book. He stated, "It is not only worthy of honor, it turns out it is a page turner. It's not often one can say that of a scholarly work. As I read, I felt as if I were transported to the Florence of 1818."

As I looked up to meet his gaze, I viewed the mirror image of Percy Shelley. After I recovered, I invited him to sit at our table. We chatted long after dinner and the awards ceremony about our teaching positions and our great passion for English Romantic poets, especially Shelley.

* * *

Soon we met again and again over lattes, over drinks, over romantic dinners. Every time I was with him, I could not shake my impression that he was like Percy on so many levels. The looks, the voice, the mannerisms, the mind, the soul—the whole package seemed like Percy.

For our first Starbucks date, we met at none other than the place where Janelle and I had many heart-to-hearts, especially about my love for a dead poet. Duncan and I sat outside at a table with a perfect view of Lake Minnetonka and its walking trails.

With the balmy temperatures of early summer, Duncan and I couldn't resist a walk partway around shimmering Lake Minnetonka, one of the largest and most beautiful among Minnesota's 10,000.

"I hope you don't think I am too bold to say this on our first official date. I sense a link of our souls and a mutual obsession with the literary, especially poetry of the Romantics. But it's more than that. It's our shared response to those poets, and to the many ways they lauded the beauty of romance—intellectually, spiritually, emotionally. They define the sum and substance of our whole selves."

Duncan left me speechless. Recovering, I said, "You have just elucidated what I have thought and felt since we met. It's as if we have twin souls."

* * *

Duncan was not all work and no play. Joining other professors from St. Thomas and St. Catherine's at a local St. Paul pub became a weekly event. I conceded my penchant for the perfect word choice by describing this time as great fun.

At one gathering, I experienced déjà vu. Drinking games turned literary in Duncan's capable hands. "Let's take turns switching a scene from one piece of literature or play to another, using pantomimes and possibly dialogue. First to guess the pieces of literature, buys us all a round."

This was too much. The only way I could describe it was a transplant of life scenes from past to present.

* * *

Dinners by candlelight with Duncan were magical, in restaurants reflecting the gentleness, charm, and romance of another time. I must admit our conversations could grow a bit scholarly, but always fascinating and exhilarating.

Our dates were made with greater frequency, from weekly to daily. Within a month of meeting, we'd both declared our love for one another.

One night over dinner, Duncan, eyes lit by candles, took my hand in his, drew it to his lips, kissing it tenderly and turning it palm upward to cover it with moist kisses. "When did you first know that you loved me?" Duncan pressed his point.

"When I turned to meet you at the awards ceremony. And it was sealed as we spoke of Shelley and his works long into the night."

"It was the same for me. So, you see, dearest Angelica, this is our destiny."

Two weeks later, he proposed over dinner in the Saint Paul Hotel, which in its historical elegance appears to be from another time.

His dark, soulful eyes met mine. He took my hand and gently kissed it. He pulled from his pocket a small box covered in a green velvet similar to the gown I wore with Percy in 1818 Florence. Opening the box, he presented to me a ring of the deepest emerald green. Not only was the moment tender and joyful, it was without a doubt, magical.

Even mystical, as Duncan stated, "Will you say yes to a poor professor and fledgling poet, rather than a wealthy poet of great fame? If I wrote a novel, you would be the protagonist. If poetry or an essay, it would be about my love for you. If a play, you would be the leading lady. Please, be my leading lady."

Past blended with present. "Oh yes, yes, yes." My journey became my destination.

ABOUT THE AUTHOR

Ingrid Anderson Sampo has had six short stories published in the Rockford Review, two in LakesAlive magazine, and three in Romancing the Lakes of Minnesota anthologies. She has completed two novels, historical fiction and young adult, progressing toward publication.

Ingrid earned a Bachelor of Arts Degree from Concordia College, Moorhead, MN, and has taught English literature and writing. She has studied under authors Jonis Agee, Faith Sullivan, Mary Sharratt, and Alison McGhee at The Loft Literary Center, Minneapolis, MN. Ingrid has attended two Loft Novel Writing Conferences, Minneapolis, MN; four Bloomington (MN) Writer's Festivals; a Minneapolis Writer's Workshop Conference; and The Flathead River Writers Conference, Kalispell, MT. She currently writes grant proposals, plans appeals, fundraising events and capital campaigns as a Fund Development professional.

Published short stories include:

Lakes Alive magazine
The Long-fingered Woman – Winter 2003
Incident at the Tom Thumb – Spring-Summer 2003

Rockford Review literary magazine
Crimes of the Heart—Summer-Fall 2004
Sleight of Hand—Summer-Fall 2005
American Geisha – Winter-Spring 2005
Daisy—Summer-Fall 2006
Nordic Craftiness—Summer-Fall 2008
A New and Improved Lutefisk—Winter-Spring 2016

Romancing the Lakes of Minnesota anthologies
Loon Racing—Romancing the Lakes of Minnesota~ Summer
Cup a' Java—Romancing the Lakes of Minnesota ~ Fall
Power to the Sixties—Romancing the Lakes of Minnesota ~ Winter

SPRING THAW
Diane Wiggert

Lower Hay Lake - Pequot Lakes, MN

"The turn is on the left." Joy Givens didn't even look up from her novel as she gave directions to her husband, Paul.

"Don't you think I know that? I've been coming to this place for close to twenty-three years," he snapped as he turned on the blinker.

His snippy tone didn't even make her flinch anymore. After twenty-two years of marriage, some of them rocky, she was used to his quick temper. Although, the flashes of anger came more frequently these last two years. Ever since Rachel started working for him.

No. I'm not going there. I am not bringing that little hussy along on our vacation.

As they pulled into the dirt driveway, Joy closed her book and turned her attention to the little cabin in front of them. It needed some stain and a few new shakes on the roof, but the feeling of comfort and contentment washed over her as she looked at their home away from home. This cabin has been in her family for over fifty years. She and Paul purchased it from her parents ten years back, when her parents decided to travel the country in a forty-foot motorhome.

Paul got out of the car, slammed the door behind him then proceeded to grab his bag—only *his* bag— from the backseat, slammed the back door as well, and walked toward the cabin.

Heaving a sigh, she unbuckled her seatbelt. This vacation was to rekindle the love and passion in their marriage and to work out their problems.

Right. This is going to be a long week.

She grabbed as much as her arms would hold before closing the door and making her way up the flagstone path. Paul, who had already unlocked the door and gone inside, was flipping on lights and checking the heat. Temperatures might climb into the seventies during the day, but the nights could drop down into the thirties. This early in the season, most people didn't open up their cabins yet. It had been a mild spring so far, and the thought of having a week with no neighbors was perfect.

"Joy. Joy, is that you?" A voice flowed over the hedge to find her. "I didn't know you and Paul would be coming up so soon."

Almost no neighbors.

"Mrs. Harvey, hello."

Shit.

The older woman was the one full-time resident on this side of the lake. She was a nice enough lady, but boy was she nosy. Paul said she was just lonely and he was probably right, but she was in no mood to entertain the older woman. Hastening her step, she entered the cabin, and closed the door behind her. Not that it would slow Judy Harvey down much. Her mother's best friend decided years ago that friends were welcome in each other's homes at any time, without knocking. Joy would have to remember to lock the door if she wanted a little privacy.

Joy could hear the furnace spooling up as she set the bag of groceries down on the counter. After putting a week's worth of food away, she carried her bag into the master bedroom. Paul's clothes still sat in his bag by the bed. She debated leaving them for him to put away. Old habits die hard, so she filled the dresser with both their clothes before she picked up her book and headed out to the deck.

The sun was low in the sky. It reflected off the calm waters of Lower Hay Lake. She loved coming up here in the spring. The days were warm, but the nights were cold, which meant no bugs, yet. It had been spring the first time she and Paul came up to the cabin alone. She remembered the long days fishing and sunbathing on the dock, and the even longer nights cuddled up by the fireplace. The first time they made love was in this very cabin.

"Joy! Where did you put the matches? How can I light the water heater if I can't find the goddamn matches?" Paul yelled from inside.

"They're in the cabinet to the right of the hot water heater. On the top shelf," she hollered back.

"I don't see them."

Things were different now. Setting her book aside, she went to get the matches. The days of cute pet names, of constantly touching one another, even if it was just to rest his hand on her back as they sat at the table or to have his leg brushing against hers, were gone. Yup, long gone. Now, the more space between them the better it seemed. She couldn't remember the last time he'd held her hand, or asked about her day and truly wanted to hear about it.

Working on their marriage seemed an insurmountable task. This week would tell them if this was a bump in the road or a dead end.

* * *

Paul Givens didn't have a clue why he'd agreed to this week at the cabin. Joy certainly didn't want to be here with him. The whole three hours driving up, she either had her nose in that damn book or was telling him what to do. *Turn here. Look out for the car on your left. Slow down, this is a speed trap.* Like he was a child, not a grown man. He really wished he knew what was stuck in her craw. Over the last couple of years, Joy had become more and more distant. He could admit that with the start of his consulting company, he dealt with a ton of stress and might have been short with her. His attempts to make it up to her all failed miserably. It was as if she'd given up on their marriage and was just going through the motions. Tired of it, he wanted his wife back and he wasn't sure if that could happen.

"Paul, are you blind?" Joy said as she came into the room and pushed past him. "I said the top shelf in the cabinet. Not on the open shelf."

She opened the cabinet and reached up. A scream tore from her throat as she wrenched her hand back and launched herself into his arms.

"Joy? What is it?" Paul's protective instinct kicked in, and he pulled her close.

Shaking her head, she hid her face in his shirt. Paul tipped his face down and inhaled the floral scent of her shampoo. He loved the smell of her, and the way she fit against his body. The contentment of having his wife in his arms made him momentarily forget the reason for the occasion.

"Something… furry," she stuttered out against his chest. "Up there." She pointed at the cabinet but didn't lift her head.

"Okay. Let me look." But as Paul moved to look, Joy didn't. She actually clung tighter. He knew well of his wife's fears—mice, snakes, even their daughter's pet guinea pig had sent her into tears when it had escaped its cage a time or two.

"Honey, I have to look. Don't worry, I'll take care of whatever it is." Paul's voice was so tender, he surprised himself. *Has it really been that long since I used a gentle tone with her?*

She stepped back and he went to the cabinet and carefully opened the door. The carcass of a mouse lay on the shelf. He picked up an old newspaper from a nearby table, wrapped up the little guy, and proceeded to take him out to the trash.

As he closed the lid on the can, he jumped. "Mrs. Harvey, you startled me." The old woman had the stealth of a ninja.

"Good day, Paul. I saw your lovely wife earlier. I tried to catch her to see how her parents are, but she must not have heard me as she went inside."

More like, she didn't want to hear you. Mrs. Harvey was a nice woman, but she drove his wife batty.

"They're doing well. Last week, they were in the Grand Canyon and now they're heading up to Wyoming to visit with Frank for a while. His wife, Molly, just gave them a new grandbaby. I believe that makes five for them."

"Well, that's just wonderful. Little Joey was born last November, making nine for me." She beamed.

Paul talked for a couple more minutes before tying up the niceties and waving goodbye to the neighbor. As he entered the cabin, he hoped to find his wife in the same state he'd left her.

Wanting to hug him close and in a tender mood. *No such luck*, he thought as she stalked by him, resumed her position on the deck, and picked up her book.

* * *

Joy roused from her novel as the back door squeaked open. She jumped when it slammed shut a moment later. She was determined not to engage her husband. Not until she could put these soft feelings in her chest away. The melting of her heart was accompanied by tiny cracks, as she realized she didn't have exclusive rights to his embrace anymore. The little tramp at the office was getting her fair share of Paul lately, she was sure of it.

"I'm going to put the dock in. Could you help me? Please?" He must have seen her roll her eyes, or he wouldn't have added the please.

"Let me change my shoes and I'll be down."

She watched as he started down the lawn to the lake, stripping off his shirt as he went. The sun glinted off his broad shoulders. She hadn't realized how much he had bulked up this last year. She'd noticed his weight loss, but it had been months since she'd seen his bare back. The contours of his shoulders flowed smoothly down his muscled back to his trim waist. His shorts were loose and rode low on his hips. Joy found herself licking her lips before she remembered he hadn't worked out for her.

Could she get over the hurt? Could she trust him? If they were really going to save their marriage, she had to put these feeling behind her. But jumping his bones would solve nothing if they didn't talk it out first. She needed to confront him once and for all. The fear of knowing for sure was more terrifying than speculation. Oh, the signs were there—late nights, a sudden desire to get in shape, a new haircut. She could smell Rachel on his clothes. Did he think she was stupid? She didn't need to be a genius to see; it was all there in black and white.

This got her nowhere. She took a deep breath and headed into the cabin for her flip-flops.

Paul had just pulled on the waders when she stopped at the water's edge. "Great, can you lift the other side and help me guide it in?"

With both of them working together, they were able to wheel the heavy aluminum decking into the lake. Water lapped over Joy's toes and she squealed, "Cold!" The dock started to slip from her fingers as she jumped back to dry land.

"Joy! Set it down." His tone was scolding. She waited for the explosion that was sure to follow but was surprised when he took in a cleansing breath, exhaled, then asked in a calm voice, "Are you all right?"

Dumbstruck for a moment, she wasn't sure how to respond, so she mutely nodded. His temper had been shorter than a flea's legs since he'd started his company.

Paul moved to the end of the dock. "Thanks for your help. I think I can get it from here if you could just guide me."

"You can't lift that alone, I can…" Her words fell away as she watched him pick up the dock like a wheelbarrow and move it deeper into the water. Her mouth dropped open as her eyes canvased the hard muscles flexing across his torso as he worked. Was this her husband? The same man she pestered for years about eating right and watching his blood pressure? The one who'd always had a few extra pounds around the middle? His toned body glistened in the sun with sweat. *Damn, he doesn't look like a desk jockey now.*

He set the dock down and turned to her. "Thanks again. I'm going to get the boat in the water. Maybe we could go for an evening cruise tonight."

"Okay," she answered automatically, still miffed by the softening in his attitude. She hoped it wasn't a trick to get her out in the middle of the lake so he could ask for a divorce where no one could hear them arguing. Or worse, to strangle her and then drop her body into the deepest part of the lake. She rubbed the goosebumps from her arms.

No, that was silly, she berated herself. She glanced over her shoulder as she headed back to the cabin. He was whistling.

* * *

Paul finished tying the boat to the cleat as the smell of burgers on the grill tickled his nostrils. *Joy makes a mean burger*, he thought, as his stomach growled.

The realization of his actions hit him this morning somewhere between the mouse corpse and the dock launch. He had been an ass to his wife for no reason, and he knew every action had a reaction. The only way he could to save his marriage was to start treating his wife with respect and kindness. After holding her in his arms this morning, he was sure he wanted nothing more than to repair the damage done to their relationship. He just wished he knew what had caused the rift in the first place. Yes, he worked long hours and sure, he was cranky at times, but she'd pulled away from him and he couldn't say why.

"I'm only human," he muttered as he started up the hill. It wasn't easy being sweet and loving when she quit making meals for him and turned her back on every attempt at intimacy. This weekend was their last chance and he knew it. Either they would rekindle their spark or twenty-two-years together would go up in flames.

After crossing the empty deck, he reached for the screen door and froze. Joy was grabbing a salad out of the refrigerator, her denim shorts pulled taut over her heart-shaped rear. Paul stood motionless as he tried to remember the last time he had his hands on her gorgeous ass. Too long ago.

Joy shut the fridge door and let out a startled squeal when she saw him standing in the doorway. "I hope you're hungry. Lunch is almost ready," she said once she regained her composure.

Oh, he was hungry, all right.

His eyes took in her lush pink lips and her sweet little body. *The food looks good, too*, he thought, as she walked by with his favorite strawberry salad. Joy set the food on the table before heading out to the deck. Paul watched her. She appeared flushed and acting strange. Nervous, if he wasn't mistaken.

He washed up in the sink before sitting down at the table. He jumped up when she entered carrying the tray of burgers. "Here, let me help you."

Joy stopped mid-stride and stared at him as if he had sprouted a horn in the middle of his forehead. Had it really been that long since he'd offered such common courtesies as holding doors and carrying heavy objects for her?

She was still staring at him as he went to her, so he took the opportunity to kiss her cheek as he lifted the plate from her hands. She couldn't see his grin as he set the plate on the table. *Well, if a little common kindness blew her away, this could make her faint.* He pulled out her chair and gestured for her to sit.

She didn't lose consciousness. If anything, it had the opposite effect. Joy gave him an icy glare and a chilling "Thank you" as she took her seat.

He barely had his butt in the chair when she asked, "What gives?"

"What? I can't be nice to my wife?"

She gave him one more evil eye before she started to eat. He was going to let it go, but the thought that he was trying to repair their marriage and she didn't appreciate it really rubbed him the wrong way. He set his fork down with an audible *clunk*.

"I'm making an effort. The least you could do is be civil. You proposed this week to work on our problems."

Joy jumped at his sudden fit of anger. Her brows knit together and she frowned at him for a moment before relaxing her features. "You're right. I'm sorry," she huffed out in an exasperated breath. He didn't know if she was fed up with him or the situation, but he wasn't going to argue about it if he didn't have to.

Paul picked up his fork and returned his attention to his food. Absentmindedly, he reached up to scratch an itch on his chest. Joy made a noticeable gulp. He looked up. She was just sitting there, fork hovering a few inches off her plate, looking at him. Correction, not just a casual glance, but she was staring at him. His chest to be precise.

Glancing down, he saw nothing then looked back to his wife. Her eyes still took in his bare chest. He stopped scratching and slowly, sensually moved his fingers over to his sternum then back to his pectoral. He bit his inner lip to keep from grinning as he watched her. He knew by the darkening of her eyes and the tiny gasp that escaped her parted lips that she was totally turned on. He'd worked out several mornings a week for the better part of a year and it appeared to finally be paying off.

He was just about to do the Dwayne "The Rock" Johnson Pec Pop of Love when a voice from the other room doused the mood.

"Hello? Paul? Joy?"

"Crap!" The spell was broken. Paul wished he'd thought to lock the door.

Joy snapped out of her trance. "Put a shirt on," she scolded, before rising to greet the neighbor. "Hello, Mrs. Harvey."

"Oh, lunch. Perfect timing. I brought you some of my famous banana bread."

Joy took the loaf and handed it to him. It slipped just before he set it down and hit the table with a thump. Famous, all right. Famously awful. Mrs. Harvey was a wonderful lady, but she couldn't bake to save her soul.

"Thank you, we love your baked goods," he said. *Yup, the last loaf made a great anchor.*

"You two sure have been busy this morning. I see you put the dock in the water already."

Paul waited. With anyone else, that would be the end of the statement, but not with Mrs. Harvey.

"You know, since my beloved William passed, God bless his soul, I don't get out on the lake unless my children are here."

And that was it. She was angling for a boat ride and he wasn't taking the bait.

"Paul and I were going to take the boat out for a short ride tonight. Would you care to join us?"

SPRING THAW

No. She did not just ask the nosy neighbor along on their ride tonight. He could throttle his wife. He'd hoped to sweet-talk Joy and start moving past the hurdles standing in the way of resuming a happy marriage. Or, at least, find out what the obstacles were.

"Oh my, I would love to take an evening cruise. If it's not too much trouble. The sunset is so beautiful on the water."

Joy piped up before he could tell her it was a major imposition. "No trouble. We would love to have you along."

Before he knew what had transpired, his wife and neighbor had settled on a time and walked outside onto the deck. Picking up his fork, he went back to his lunch.

It's going to be a long week.

* * *

Mrs. Harvey's presence on the boat that first night did nothing to squelch the flowing current of sexual attraction between Paul and her.

"You look cold. Take my jacket," Paul said, sliding the cotton hoodie around her shoulders as the sun set. Joy fought to contain the delicious chills that played up her spine as his fingers grazed the nape of her neck.

She spent the next two days avoiding her husband to no avail. Holding on to her anger was getting harder with every kind word and each brush of his fingers over her sensitized skin. Could she move past his indiscretions to save their marriage?

Today, the boat held only the two of them. No chaperone.

Paul cut the motor. The sun was high in the sky and temperatures reached the low seventies. He stripped off his shirt as he made his way to the front of the boat. Joy sat transfixed, her eyes glued to his broad shoulders. She watched the play of his muscles as he dropped anchor. The last three days had been worse than she could have imagined.

She managed to regain her composer before he returned to his seat. The heat was rising and she wasn't sure if it was from the sun or something deep inside her. She pulled off her cover-up and felt her husband's eyes on her breasts. *Inside, definitely inside.*

"Let me help you," he said, sunscreen in hand. His strong hands glided across her shoulder and down her arm before she could speak.

Her husband was wooing her and she knew it. At every turn, he was there, holding the door or bringing her lemonade. He used any opportunity over the last few days to touch her, and she wasn't blind to the sexy curve of his lips or the way his eyes currently trailed down her body.

Her breasts tightened with desire, betraying her. Her mind jumped ship, too. She was so close to saying the hell with his affair. She didn't know how much longer she could deny the needs of her body.

Talk. They had to talk before she gave in. She was being a coward avoiding him and she knew it. But she still didn't know if her heart could get over the affair. This was as good a place as ever to have a relationship-ending conversation.

Joy pulled away when she felt the brush of his lips on her neck. "Paul."

His eyes were so clear. An open window to his soul, she'd always thought. At the moment, he looked at her with lust, a little impatience, and…was that love? Could he still love her?

"Paul. We should…" He stepped toward her, and her words fell away as his hand glided up her arm and curled around the back of her neck.

"Honey. Yes, we need to talk." He eclipsed the sun as he leaned in. His lips hovered for a moment and his blue eyes begged her to submit. "Later."

His lips captured hers in a passionate assault. Her eyelids slid closed as she melted into him. She'd missed this, his all-consuming kisses. Joy's hands found his soft, sun-kissed hair and held him in place. Time stood still. They were in a bubble of lust. He'd always had that effect on her. One touch, one kiss, and she was clueless to anything and everything around them. So unaware of their surroundings that the motion of the boat and the sounds of a motor did nothing to chill their kiss. Only the cold spray of water from a passing speedboat broke the spell.

They pulled apart. Paul laughed, shaking the water from his hair. Joy stood stunned. Not from the wave, but from the realization of what would've happened if the chilling interruption hadn't come along. She loved her husband. That was clear. She still found him desirable. But she would hate herself if she had sex with him before clearing the air.

"Why?" She locked eyes with his, brown to blue. "Was I not enough?"

His laughter stopped. "Not enough what? Joy. Honey, what are you talking about?" He reached for her hand and she stepped back, almost falling overboard.

"No!" she shouted as he moved in to help her. "Don't touch me." Joy sat on the bow, taking deep breaths.

"Joy?" When she didn't answer, Paul ran his hands through his hair and turned away from her. He suddenly stopped, faced her, and said, "I'm sorry. I was an ass and you have every right to be upset with me. But, Joy, I'm trying, really trying, but I'm not the only one in this marriage. You think it's easy to come home tired and hungry, to find my wife pissed off and giving me the cold shoulder?"

She didn't know what to say. He admitted he was sorry, but that was his go-to response when she was mad. She was drained and couldn't do this. Not now, not ever.

"Take me back."

He gave her a long look. For the first time, she couldn't read him. He pulled up anchor as she took her seat, then he started the boat and slowly motored back to the dock.

* * *

He watched her storm up the hill to the cabin. This was crazy. He loved his wife, and he was ninety-nine percent sure she loved him, too. He replayed their conversation in his head. "Not enough? What did she mean by that?" he muttered as he tied up the boat.

Paul hung out on the dock for a good fifteen minutes longer

than needed. He wasn't in a rush to rehash the argument. One minute, he had his wife in his arms and the next, she was staring at him with wounded brown eyes. Shaking his head, he paced the dock. He knew his apology was lame, but his brain hadn't been the prominent thinking organ at the time. She changed gears faster than a Ferrari, and he couldn't keep up. So, yes, he'd gotten mad, but he hadn't lied about being an idiot. He felt like one right now. He knew this little spat was not so small and could very well be the end of his marriage, yet he didn't have a clue what it was about.

"Damn it. I will not flush twenty-two years without a fight." Paul stomped up the hill and flung the door open. "Joy!" He moved to the bedroom when he didn't find her in the kitchen or living room.

Crap! She was packing. He took a calming breath and slowly expelled it. "Are you going somewhere?"

"I can't do this." She didn't even give him the courtesy of stopping to look at him.

That's it. They were having this out right here, right now. He moved up behind her, slid a hand around her waist, and turned her to face him. His anger melted at the sight of her tear-streaked cheeks. He lifted his hand and wiped the moisture from her face.

"Talk to me." He wanted to kiss her but knew that would be fighting dirty. "Please."

Joy didn't step back but took as much air into her lungs as possible. Paul wondered if she would ever release it, then she finally spoke.

"Why? Why did you sleep with her?"

He looked deep into her eyes. She was serious. He let her go and stumbled back, putting a few inches of space between them. "What? You think..." His mind was reeling. "I haven't had sex with anyone but you. Hell, we haven't even so much as cuddled in close to a year. Is this what this is all about? Wait. Who do you think I slept with?" Paul asked when he finally recovered from the shock.

"Rachel." Joy looked fierce standing there, hands on her hips.

Her eyes flamed, but he didn't care, anger and hurt were

bubbling inside his gut. He wasn't about to let her see the hurt so he embraced the anger. He was so pissed off by the time he responded, he couldn't give a rat's ass about staying calm.

"You really thought I was cheating on you? With Rachel?" His volume ratcheted up a notch or two as he spoke.

Nice to know she thought so little of him that she assumed he was doing the hot and nasty with his young assistant. "I should be flattered that you think a twenty-four-year-old would find me attractive. But I think her personal-trainer fiancé, who she is madly in love with, would get a little upset."

Joy's hands slipped from her hips. "But, your hair. And…" She waved a hand up and down in front of him.

"What? This?" He put his hand on his chest and ran it down his abs. "You've been harping on me for years to lose weight. You were always buying those God-awful healthy snacks."

She didn't look convinced. Moving slowly toward her, he waited for her to look up into his eyes. "I did this for you," he confessed. "You pulled away and it scared me. One day I was waiting for my barber and reading the magazines. Sports, business, the usual. I picked up a *GQ* and looked at the cover, then I looked in the mirror." He shrugged.

Joy was watching him. "So, the hair…" She played with the blond tips.

"It was for you. Why else would I let them put aluminum foil in my hair? I think I picked up a Canadian radio station for a while."

"I like it." Her lips crept up. Then her eyes moved from his hair to his chest. Her hand followed. "I like this, too."

Paul relished the feel of her hand on his stomach, but gently grabbed her wrist. When she looked up at him, he said, "Is that it? You really thought I was having an affair?"

Tears filled her eyes and her lower lip trembled. She nodded before looking away. Her whispered apology tore at his heart. All this time, the pain and suffering could have been avoided.

"But you believe me?"

Joy looked into his eyes, not speaking for a minute, and then she nodded. "Yes."

"I want you to know," he said, taking her face in his hands, "I will never, ever cheat on you. You are the one. *My* one. Until death do us part, remember?"

Tears freely flowed down her cheeks now. "Yes, I remember. I love you, Paul."

He kissed her then. "I love you, and only you."

* * *

The lights were out, but the car sat on the gravel driveway and the boat bobbed in the rhythmic waves at the dock. Judy Harvey never considered knocking as she entered the cabin. She would just leave the cookies on the table. *They must be out on a walk*. Paul and Joy were such a nice couple, Judy had to make them some of her famous oatmeal cookies to thank them for taking her out on the boat.

If her senses were correct, the young pair was having a little trouble. And after forty-seven years of marriage, she knew that sweets always smoothed the road to reconciliation. Her William was much more amenable if he had something sweet first.

Soft voices came from the other room. So, they were home. *Good*, she thought, she'd just stick her head in and say good evening. The voices grew louder as she reached the kitchen. The plate of cookies was halfway to the table when a loud groan came from the next room. It was followed by a soft moan.

The treats slid off the plate. Judy let them drop as her hand automatically rose to her heart. "Oh, my," she whispered as she turned to leave, giving the couple their privacy.

She smiled. Maybe she would knock next time. Or not.

ABOUT THE AUTHOR

Diane Wiggert writes contemporary romances. Her love of home improvement projects has her continually sanding, staining or painting something in her home, to her family's dismay. Someday, her home projects will be done, and she will have more time for her other love, reading.

She lives in a small Minnesota town with her husband, son, and crazy canine. *Spring Thaw* is her third short story. Her other works include *Magic at Moose Lake* and *Love's No Joke*, found in *The Romancing the Lakes of Minnesota Anthologies- Autumn and Winter* editions.

You can follow Diane on Facebook or Twitter.

TAKE YOUR SHIRT OFF & STAY FOREVER
Lanna Farrell

Shirt Lake - Deerwood, MN

Reagan Tierney gripped the steering wheel tightly. Her shoulders and neck were stiff, her head throbbing. She blamed it on the late-night darkness, fog, and glare from the headlights of on-coming traffic stabbing her eyes.

Inside the car, it was dark and lonely, with only her radio to keep her company. She glanced over at her phone lying on the passenger seat. Should she call someone? Her dad, perhaps? *Nah, it's too late.*

Why in the hell had she started a mini trip up north this late at night? With the mountain of manuscripts piled on her desk and too many deadlines looming, Reagan had begun to question her own sanity—*that's why.*

She couldn't come up with an excuse, still, for leaving Minneapolis this late at night to drive through none other than God's country. The wildlife alone was dangerous, never mind the ice and potential for snow at any given time this early in the spring. It was a joke among her family; her father had said April's weather was as finicky as a woman changing clothes or shoes when getting ready for a date.

She grabbed her cell phone and looked to make sure no last minute emails or phone calls had come in. The coverage was sporadic at the best. Over the past month, she and her partners had planned and organized a conference for writers and readers. The past few days had kicked her ass.

On top of all that, her lead cover model had canceled at the last second due to an illness. Reagan was overwhelmed from the stress to find a replacement. It's not like she could pick up her phone, dial 1-800-Gorgeous. Trying to cold call a male model this late in the planning stage would be impossible. The models she worked with had schedules out for, at least, a month or more.

Still, Reagan fully intended to pull that rabbit out of her hat by

Sunday. Though, she had started to doubt herself, because she had yet to accomplish a thing through research, social media, or her vast network of people for covers and models.

Reagan peeked in her rearview mirror. A car's headlights lit the back seat and showed her laptop and notebooks sprawled all over. This only confirmed to her how serious she was about her work. The only thing she had to remove herself from the fast pace of Minneapolis was the lake home up north. She needed the space to regroup and help her mind slow enough to achieve her goal.

She knew a few of the models personally who had already signed up. She would call them and see if they had friends who'd join them for the conference. Even though it was a full six days, the models didn't need to be there until Wednesday and stay through the last day, Saturday. With the model found, she'd be okay and the conference would go forward without a hiccup. She just had to remain positive, be optimistic.

"Yeah, right." She pounded the steering wheel. "Stupid is more like it!" she yelled, thankful no one in the world could hear.

She shook her head, wiped the stray tear that slipped from her eye, and moved her head and neck around. With her hand, she massaged her shoulder muscles to see if she could loosen up and enjoy the drive instead of panicking every time something crossed the road in front of her.

To help distract her from the looming black road and the wretchedness of her life, she let her eyes focus on the white line of the highway as it clicked by like the secondhand of a clock.

* * *

Reagan stopped in Zimmerman a while back to buy an energy drink and a large cup of coffee to combat the sleepiness overtaking her brain. The five-minute rest had rejuvenated her enough to continue on the trip.

Now, forty-five minutes later, she chuckled at the realization she needed to find a bathroom. *Geez, girly, way too much caffeine. You're tweaking!*

Hearing a favorite song, she reached over and turned up the radio. Singing along while trying to forget there wasn't a rest area or gas station for miles, she was riding high from all the stimulated energy. Reagan's finger tapped the steering wheel as she screamed the chorus at the top of her lungs.

The car lurched sideways. Her body hit the driver's door, and the sounds of metal crunching and glass breaking drowned out the radio.

Reagan had a moment of panic when her seatbelt tightened across her chest. Her head hit hard against something, the instant pain throbbed throughout her brain, creating a moment of blackness. Time stood still for a second then sped by as the steering wheel whipped to the left, causing her to lose her grip and the ability to straighten out the car.

She felt the car jerk again as it hit something that sent it careening off the road. Her vision blurred as the car slid down an embankment, and then she could only see darkness before it hit something hard, slamming her body one last time against the driver's door.

Heart pounding, Reagan's hand shook as she touched the driver's window. A white blanket of snow obstructed any view. Her voice rattled as she prayed, "Thank you, Lord, for letting me live."

She took inventory of her body, slowly feeling for broken bones, gushing blood, or serious injuries. She didn't appear to be too bad off, just battered and bruised.

Reagan looked out the windows and saw nothing but blackness. The blood rushed to her face as her heart pounded rapidly, adrenaline taking her by storm as she realized she had crashed her car and was stuck in the middle of nowhere.

The radio still blared, shattering the silence she now craved. Pushing the knob, she shut off the music, and to her relief, heard the engine's sweet purr.

Her heart racing, she was on the verge of hyperventilating. She needed to calm down. A self-talk was what she needed the most. *Breathe, Reagan, you're okay.*

She was relieved to find she'd landed in a pile of snow, which had probably saved her life. Reagan had seen fatalities when people hit deer or livestock.

She wanted to get out and see where she'd landed so, she first tried the driver's door. It opened an inch, which caused the light to turn on inside but it hurt her eyes. There was no way she could get out through the inch or so space she'd earned for her efforts. But Reagan could see that the entire driver's side of the car was buried in the snow.

The stress of the accident and not knowing how to get out of the ditch took its toll on her emotions. Inhaling a deep, relaxing breath, she knew the mind could play tricks on a person. People were taught to drive but not how to make reasonable decisions after an accident.

In April, the snow was wet and heavy, but the temperatures outside were probably near the thirties. She should be safe from freezing to death, even if she was stuck out here overnight. Possibly even longer if she was careful. Picking up her cell, she looked down to see she had no service.

"Figures." She threw the device into her purse. "Now what?"

She needed to conserve energy. Spring in the northern part of Minnesota could turn deadly in a manner of minutes with the indecisive weather. But her mind, again, was playing tricks on her. If she shut off the car, she knew it would feel as if she'd shut off her life support.

"Stop it!" she yelled. Freaking out about this wasn't helping her at all. Quickly, before she had a chance to change her mind, she shut down the car.

She leaned her aching head back and closed her eyes, just for a few moments. Relaxing only caused her body to ache more, so Reagan took a deep breath and decided to take matters into her own hands.

After she grabbed her coat from the back seat, she draped it over herself to keep her body's warmth contained.

Her mini-vacation had just turned into a huge nightmare. No cell coverage and it was too late at night for anyone else to be on the road.

She prayed someone would drive by and see her car.

Two Hours later

Relief flooded her as red, blue, and white lights appeared to strobe through her car. Then headlights and a spotlight lit up the area and she could see exactly where her car had landed. She let out the breath she'd been holding for a few short seconds, when she had thought it might be a serial killer or something. She moaned and laid her head back. She was an author and had a vivid imagination, but she needed to put those thoughts out of her mind.

Her savior was clearly a police officer. The only thing she'd get out of tonight would be a scenario for another story. Her patience dwindled as she waited for the person to get to her. It seemed to take forever but she knew, in reality, only a few minutes passed before he tapped on the passenger window, his flashlight blinding her.

Shielding her vision with her hand, she asked, "Can you please shut that off?"

"Oh, sorry," the deep, male voice apologized, and the light instantly turned away.

After she turned the car on, she rolled down the window.

He asked, "Ma'am, you okay?"

"I think so," she answered, still not seeing his face clearly. She was not prepared for him to lean inside through the passenger window and touch her chin, tilting her head sideways.

"It looks like you hit your head."

"It's a little sore, but it seems to be okay." When she touched it, there was a flash of pain and she saw a small amount of blood on her hand. "Oh dang," she murmured.

"Yep, you have a nasty cut." He pointed to her forehead. "Right there."

"It only hurts a little. I didn't even feel it. Weird."

"It'll hurt worse in the morning, I promise." His deep voice was gentle to her ears.

He moved around her car, stumbling slightly, and Reagan realized he was treading through deep snow.

When he came back to her open window, he peeked in and said, "Look, I'm not sure how to get you out. But, maybe we should wait for an EMT to look you over first."

"Why? I'm sore all over, but I can get out of here and walk up to your car if you need me to?" Panic of being left alone, even for a few moments, seemed to control her thoughts more than the idea of waiting for the others to arrive and take a look at her.

"Look, I just want to make sure you don't have any other injuries. Hang on for one minute, I'll be back." He stepped away from her car and appeared to be talking into the radio near his ear.

Only a few short moments went by before the officer leaned back inside her passenger door. "You doing okay in here?"

"I'm good. Honestly, my body is sore, but it's all in my muscles. Nothing is broken, I promise." She moved her neck around, up and down, showing him she was okay.

"If you're sure, we can try getting you out and up to my car where it's warm." He tugged on the door, but it was stuck. "But I'm really not sure how to get you out of this car. The door is jammed up with snow."

Reagan attempted to lean toward the passenger side and hit her leg on the steering column. "Dang it!"

He pointed. "Can you get out through the driver's door?"

She shook her head. "Already tried but the door won't budge. The only way out is from the passenger side."

"Just ease your body up onto to the seat, then slide over."

She nodded. "I'll try."

Using the steering wheel, she pulled herself up onto the seat. Legs tucked under her butt, she sat there for a second to assess her next move. She inhaled a few short breaths and peeked out the window. The officer was kicking snow away from the path of the door. Slowly, she worked her way across the car, bumping her knee on the shifter in the process.

"Stupid little car. Dang it! *Ouch*."

He pulled the door, opening it, creating just enough room for her small frame to slip through. Holding onto her elbow, he helped her ease out the car.

"Oh, wait, I have to get my purse." She reached in and grabbed her bag off the floor.

"Okay, ready?" he asked with authority, holding her steady until she gained her footing.

"Yep, thanks." The first few steps went okay, until her feet sank about a foot deep in the snow. "Damn!" she screamed, frustration mounting. She didn't want to admit to him that her body had been fine, but once she got out and started to move, the soreness was hindering her.

"Hang on." He lifted her up into his arms.

Reagan grabbed ahold of him, his arms large and solid. This man worked out. She could tell he was strong and fit as he settled her against his body.

His sure-footed boots stomped through the deep snow. A foot of snow turned to mere inches then melted into a thin sheet as they neared the shoulder. After he set her down on the pavement, he continued to hold on to her to prevent her from slipping and falling.

When she looked up, she realized how tall he was. His large-boned shape filled in the heavy coat he wore.

He put his arm around her shoulders and pulled her tightly against his body. His jacket opened, allowing her to see inside. He wore a t-shirt that peeked through the top three buttons of his police issued blue dress shirt. On top of that, he wore a down vest under the heavy black winter coat. She wanted to touch every inch of his lean, dark skin—his entire body—before he let her go.

Reagan fought to control her almost wandering hands, but it took some effort. Even more so when she tried to step away and he refused to let her go.

Her body pressed against his voluntarily. And when his hands held onto her longer than necessary, she certainly didn't care. As a matter of fact, she enjoyed the warmth and comfort because it continued to soothe her trembling body.

His aftershave tickled her nose and made her body come alive in places she didn't want it to, at least not right then. She'd been in an accident, the man was a cop, her body was sore as hell, and she had a head wound. Not the time to have sexual tension coiling inside her body.

Reagan took a deep breath and tried to step away. When her hands met his chest, she stopped, not quite ready to move.

Waiting a few moments, she looked up and smiled, "I'm okay, you can probably let me go."

"You sure? Let's try walking. My car is across the highway."

As they walked, he continued to hold onto her. Her foot slipped and she almost went down, but before her knee hit the ground, he caught ahold of her body and picked her back up.

She sighed, "Well, then, not so smooth, am I?"

"Hey, no worries, it's really slippery out here tonight."

Once they finished shuffling their way to the car, he opened the door for her. Instead of getting in, she looked up. His profile spoke of power and ageless strength. His face bronzed from the sun, the darkness only added to his good looks.

He cleared his throat, and said, "When you're done doing what you're doing, can I offer you my warm patrol car until we can get you help?"

Reagan didn't even realize she'd been studying him. Quick with wit herself, she teased him back with a soft chuckle. "Wait, almost done."

Not missing the humor in the situation, the officer threw back his head and let out a boisterous laugh, adding to her own.

"Can I ask you something?"

"Sure?"

"It's the wrong time of the year for a tan. What's up with that?" Relaxing immensely, she slipped from his warm embrace and slid into the front seat.

"Oh, I went to Mexico on vacation a couple weeks ago. Spent almost the entire week outside."

After closing her door, he walked around the front of his car. The bright lights illuminated his great looks even more. His thick dark hair was tapered neatly to his collar, most of it hidden under the hat he wore. He had an air of power and the appearance of one who demanded instant obedience.

At this point, she'd do just about anything for him, so she would love to get to know him and see if he was that type of person. Always one to like a man who took charge and got the job done.

Reagan shook her head, *stop all these thoughts racing in your overactive imagination, Tierney.*

She couldn't help it. At that precise moment, she realized she'd whacked her head harder than she thought. To pick up a stranger, even a cop, was beyond her wildest dreams. Never in her life would she do that—well, maybe.

* * *

Scott O'Riley couldn't believe the beauty sitting in the front seat of his patrol car. Why was this woman making him so nervous? He was used to helping the opposite sex, what was so different about this one? He figured he'd better stay with her. At least until the ambulance arrived and they looked her over and decided if she needed to go to the hospital.

He knew the mess in the road had to be cleaned up, and a tow truck for her car was on its way. He wasn't sure how bad the damage was, but the driver would take a look and then give him an idea.

Something about her seemed familiar and he couldn't figure it out, but he intended to.

The large buck lying dead on the highway told him how hard this young lady had hit, even before her car slammed into that snow bank. He prayed he'd made the right decision by getting her out of her car.

He slid into the driver's seat. After he shut the door to keep the warmth in, he turned and asked, "How are you?" He gently touched her chin. "The wound on your head is still bleeding a little."

"I'm okay." She touched her forehead. "It is starting to hurt a little." She looked up at him with those big blue eyes.

When her body trembled lightly, he asked, "Are you cold?"

"A little." Her smile brightened her face.

He twisted his wrist and glanced at his watch. "The ambulance should be here anytime now. We'll get you checked out and figure out what to do about the car."

"Thank you. I hate being so much trouble." She shivered and given the paleness of her face, he thought she might be going into shock. "Here." He shrugged out of his jacket and placed it around her shoulders. It drowned her small-framed body, but it would help her warm up quickly.

"Thank you," she whispered, confirming she'd been cold.

He wanted to keep her mind off the worry. "I need to call in your information." He held out his hand and asked, "Do you have your license on you?"

She nodded, opening her purse, and handed him her ID.

Reading her information, his heart lurched. He looked at her. "Are you *the*...?"

"*The*?" She tilted her head, looking at him oddly.

"*The* Reagan Tierney? *Alphabet Murders* Tierney?" He couldn't believe what a dork he was.

"Oh, yeah!" She smiled brightly; her face completely animated by her excitement.

He couldn't believe it. He had the famous author Reagan Tierney sitting in his car.

* * *

"My mom and sister would go nuts if they knew. They've read every one of your romance and mystery novels."

"That's so sweet. I have a book or two in my car." She nodded in the direction of her wrecked vehicle.

"Yeah, that's a problem. I think I'll have to wait." He grinned. "You know, your *Alphabet* books kept me from falling asleep many nights while I sat out here on duty."

"You don't say? I'm flattered, Officer, really."

"Please, the name is Scott."

She was flattered and wanted to get to know him better. She stuck out her hand. "Scott, it's an honor to meet you. I have my new release with me. It hasn't been released yet. But, I think I can help you out, I happen to know the author," she teased.

His smile brightened his face and blue eyes. He spoke as he typed in his computer. "The *S* one right?"

She chuckled. "Wow, I'm impressed. You even know which one is due to release in May."

"We're almost the same age." He handed her back her license.

"Really? When's your birthday?" she asked. He didn't look a day over twenty-five. People aged differently. She'd learned that working her way through college as a bartender.

"September ninth, same year as you."

"No way. You don't look thirty," she complimented easily.

"I am and you definitely don't look your age. I figured you to be in your early twenties." He winked at her, and they laughed together.

"Well, I think we both look younger than we are." Reagan liked the easy way they bantered back and forth.

"I'll definitely agree with that statement." He laughed before asking her, "So, Reagan, tell me a little about you? What made you decide to be a writer?"

She was definitely flattered by his interest. "Well, let me see. As a young teenager, I hid away and read books all the time. As I reached my high school years, I started writing a few short stories, and continued on into college. When my teacher challenged me to write a book, *Alphabet A Murder* was developed."

"Seriously?"

"You know; it was by total accident I was able to be a success. I don't take it for granted, though. I appreciate every reader and fan I've gotten over the years. Tell me about you, please."

"Well, like what do you want to know?"

Reagan wanted to know everything but decided to start small.

"What made you decide to go into law enforcement?"

"Well, my father and grandfather are both police officers. I didn't always want to be one, it was something I decided when I blew out my knee during tenth grade in varsity football. My dream of going pro was over."

"I'm sorry, that's too bad. Your knee?"

"It's all good. Silly pipe dream of football anyways. I really enjoy being a cop." His gaze dropped from her eyes, to her shoulders, to her breasts.

Her body warmed up from the attention. She needed to ask because she knew her interest was more than infatuation or curiosity. Reagan's body wanted him in ways that she'd need to go to confessional for.

"Scott, are you married?" She covered her mouth. She knew her face had turned bright red.

"Hey, no you don't. Not allowed to be embarrassed, that was a fair question. No I'm not married, and I have no one waiting for me." He touched her cheek lightly with the back of his hand.

"That was too forward, even for me. But, I just needed to know." She felt an eager affection coming from him.

"Well, Reagan, that's fair. Now it's my turn to ask you something."

She nodded, "Of course."

Leaning in closer, he asked, "Are you married or is there someone special waiting for you?"

She shook her head. "Nope and no."

"That's a good thing, because, I think I want to kiss you," he whispered.

She nodded then leaned into him. He helped her by cupping his hand behind her neck and gently pulling her even closer to him. His mouth next to hers, she could even feel his breath. Reagan closed her eyes, praying he'd take the initiative and just go for it. But, suddenly, he released her and pulled back. They'd been interrupted by lights coming their way.

"Well, I'm sorry to say, we're being interrupted by the ambulance." He reached over and touched her face. "I'd really like to talk with you, maybe over dinner or coffee?"

"Sure, I'd like that." He was a really nice man and easy to talk to. She didn't want this special moment to end. "Scott?"

"Yeah?" He'd opened the door and stepped out.

"Thank you, I'm going to hold you to dinner." The words ran out of her mouth.

"I expect you to." He held his clipboard up. "Can I get your phone number off this?"

"Of course." She smiled, the excitement causing her stomach to tighten. She lifted her hand to wave, but he'd already gotten out of the car and was walking toward the ambulance.

* * *

The cold, damp mist and fog of early spring greeted him as he walked out into the night air to help the emergency vehicles lining the road. The night glowed with lights from the ambulance and fire trucks.

Scott led Dave and Mike, both paramedics, over to the passenger side of his squad car. He opened the door. "Reagan, this is Dave and Mike, they want to take care of you."

She nodded. "Hi."

Instead of waiting with her, he walked over to the tow truck. "Hey, Wayne, how's it going?"

"Hey, Scott, I'm good. You?" Wayne grabbed a hold of the cinch in the front of the truck and started walking toward the car.

Scott asked, "How's the wife and kiddos?"

"Oh, they're good. Wife's pregnant again." Wayne and he had gone to school together. His wife, Heidi, had been in their grade, as well.

"Number four?"

"Yeah, I guess that would be accurate." Wayne laughed as he walked the line down to Reagan's car.

Not needed at the car, Scott headed back to see how Reagan was doing. Mike was walking beside her.

"Hey, you decided to go to the hospital?"

Reagan smiled. "Yeah, Mike, here thinks I might need stitches."

Mike helped her up into the ambulance. Scott leaned up against the rear of the vehicle. "Is it okay if I call you?" He held up his cell. "To let you know about your car, as soon as it is pulled out of the ditch?"

She smiled. "Sure, that would be great."

He waved. "See you soon."

He turned to walk away, when he heard her yell out, "Scott?"

He spun on his heel facing her. "Yeah?"

"Thank you!" He caught her wave as Dave slammed the doors and walked around to the front of the ambulance.

He watched the ambulance drive away. When he turned to check on Wayne, his friend stood there grinning.

Scott asked, "What?"

"You got it bad, buddy."

Scott wasn't sure he'd heard Wayne right. "Sorry, what did you say?"

"Never mind, I can see for myself. She must be someone pretty special." Wayne nodded toward the car he'd pulled up onto the road.

Scott laughed, but Wayne had given him a lot to think about.

A few hours later

The hospital buzzed with commotion, people rushing everywhere. Scott walked with purpose toward the emergency room. His stomach felt the butterflies of nerves. He wondered if she'd welcome him, or think he was too forward. He wanted to make sure she had a way home, didn't he?

He headed to the nurses' station, finding another friend manning the desk. "Hey, Amanda, I'm looking for Reagan Tierney?"

"Oh, she's over there in room seven. Come on, follow me."

He trailed after Amanda to find Reagan sitting on the edge of a gurney fully dressed. A butterfly bandage sealed the wound on her head.

She waved and greeted him with a smile. "Hi, Scott."

Relaxing a bit, he knew he'd made the right decision in coming here tonight. Her smile was bright and welcoming. He decided to go even further in his pursuit.

Winking playfully, he greeted her. "Hi, beautiful, how are you?"

Instead of the reaction he'd expected, she stirred uneasily, looked down at her hands, and answered him. "I'll live."

He gently touched her hands, stilling them. "Okay, now tell me the truth, Reagan."

Her mouth curved into an involuntary smile. "No, I guess it isn't really okay. I don't have anyone even physically near here to come and get me. My car is…"

Her blue eyes were full of life, pain, and unquenchable warmth. He wanted to enlighten her as far as her car was concerned but wasn't sure if telling her about the damage now would be wise.

She murmured, "I don't know what I'm going to do."

"Hey, Scott. How are you?" Dr. William Everett, one of his best friends, patted his back.

"I'm good, you?" Scott pulled Bill into a hug, patting him on the back.

"Busy. I volunteered this weekend because Nicky's out-of-town, now I regret it. This place is crazy. Gone into code black once tonight."

"Yeah, I noticed, this is unusual for such a small town. Well, I can help get this room open for you." He turned to Reagan. "I'm off duty, and I can take you home. If you'd like."

"Yeah, that would be great. The lake home is about fifteen minutes from here." She looked at the doctor. "How about it, doc,

TAKE YOUR SHIRT OFF & STAY FOREVER

am I good to go?"

"Well, let's take a look and see." Bill pulled a light from his pocket before asking, "Scott, give us a minute, please?"

Reagan spoke up quickly just as he turned away. "No, Scott, stay, please...?"

Surprised, he readily agreed. He leaned against the wall, his foot up against it. "Sure, I'll stay."

Bill looked her over then nodded. "I think you're doing well. Tomorrow morning, you might be a little sore from the accident, especially right across the chest where you have a slight bruise from the seatbelt. Other than that, you should be okay. I'll give you a prescription for pain. You can fill it at the med's machine in the waiting room. Anything else, Reagan, you can always call."

"Thanks, doctor." Reagan's smile grew as she stood up. "I'm ready when you are, Scott."

His heart thumped faster in his chest as she stepped closer. The scent of vanilla mixed with strawberry wafted from her. He stuck out his elbow. "After you, Reagan."

She grabbed ahold of his bent arm as they started out of the hospital.

She touched his elbow and looked up at him. He smiled. Something more than compassion but less than love seemed to take its place between them. His body reacted to her smile, laugh, and even her frown. Reagan Tierney was dangerous, but he'd lived a life of loneliness for far too long.

When his girlfriend died after a drunk driver struck her car nearly three years ago, Scott thought his life had ended as well. With Reagan, he'd actually started to feel alive.

* * *

Reagan couldn't believe her good fortune. Going into a ditch might have been the change she needed. As she rode next to Scott in his patrol car, he turned to her. "Where to, my lady?"

The question actually caused her heart to skip a beat. His presence gave her serenity and bliss she'd thought dead a long time ago. As they headed toward her parents' lake home, she tried hard to listen to her heart and body.

"Scott, you're absolutely gorgeous and sexy." She placed her hand over her mouth and coughed. Her cheeks heated and she knew her face turned red.

"Well thank you, gorgeous." He laughed, before he took her hand and held it.

He was easily the most handsome man she'd ever laid eyes on. As a photographer herself, she'd taken some pictures of models for her own book covers. If she really thought about it, she couldn't remember a male model even remotely as devilishly handsome as he was.

He gave her hand a gentle squeeze, before saying, "Reagan, I'm hopelessly attracted to you. I hope you don't think that's too weird?"

Her heart soared and she couldn't believe they'd progressed to this stage in such a short time.

She knew she'd met the perfect soulmate. Of course, she had always believed in that kind of love. For a split second, she worried he didn't feel the same attraction to her as she did for him. There was no way she was interested in a booty call, no matter how handsome this man was.

But, she threw caution to the wind. "Well, I kind of like you, too."

His direct stare and open-mouthed expression startled her. Had she made a mistake and assumed way too much? Quickly, she lowered her eyes.

"Hey, Reagan, what's going on?" He reached across the car, touched her chin, and tugged it gently until she looked up at him.

Nervously, she moistened her dry lips. "Can I make you dinner sometime this weekend? I want to thank you for all your kindness."

"Sure, that would be nice, thanks." He grinned, turning his eyes back to the road.

Riverwood Hospital in Garrison was not too far from her lake home. First signs of light were coming up with the sunrise. Scott pulled the squad car over to the shoulder and put it into park.

"Is everything okay?" She wondered why he'd stopped. Reagan was anxious to get home and enjoy the sunrise from her deck facing Shirt Lake.

"Yep. Do you feel good enough to get out and watch the sun come up with me?"

Smiling, she nodded. "You read my mind. I was just thinking about that."

"Really? Well, what do you know, just another thing we have in common." Scott chuckled. He opened his car door and walked around to hers, letting her out.

She reached for his hand, and he led her to the back of the car.

"Here, let me help you." He lifted her up onto to the trunk, and then he joined her, settling in right next to her.

Never in her life could she remember a more romantic time than holding hands to watch the sunrise.

Even though she'd written romance, it was completely different from actually living it. This was more of a fairytale than even she could weave.

The first week of spring truly flowered into something beautiful for her. Scott lifted her chin to meet his eyes. Reagan wasn't prepared for the fireworks his kiss set off in her mind and body.

"Let's get you home. I think that head wound did more to your brain than we both thought." He winked at her before pulling her off the hood and into his arms then carrying her to the passenger side of the car.

She reached for the door as he set her down on the ground and whispered in her ear, "Let me get the door for you."

Instantly, she dropped her hand, and stood waiting. He opened the door, she slid in, and he shut it.

Thankful for the few moments to compose her erratic heartbeat, she waited for the hot, sexy, and—from what he'd exhibited so far—very-manly officer to get into the car. What would she do with all that testosterone? She'd figure it out before this weekend ended.

Reagan somehow knew Scott wasn't going to be a man who expected a one-night stand from her.

An idea hit her. If she asked him to be the model she needed, somehow they could try to spend some time together and see if they could build on this connection she felt growing between them.

Reagan covered her mouth, trying to hide the girlish giggle. Acting like a fourteen-year-old with her first crush wasn't her style. When he opened the door and slid in, her stomach somersaulted and she coughed to hide her nervousness.

Ah, hell. She spoke before she could change her mind. "Scott, I have a huge favor to ask?"

* * *

Scott knew she was up to something by the way she laughed and her eyes brightened. "Okay, what's up?"

He knew he would try or do anything she asked, even at this point in their newly blossoming relationship. The exciting connection they'd already established in such a short time seemed as natural as a gentle spring breeze.

"I need a cover model to come and hang out at a six-day conference next week." She grinned, her cheeks bright red.

"A what?" he coughed.

He knew he would be able to help her out since he'd already asked for next week off. Trying to get everything at home ready for spring and summer would keep him occupied the entire week.

"Forget it, bad idea." She waved her hand, turned her head, and stared out the window.

He couldn't believe she'd pretty much asked him to spend the following week with her. He thought it was cute she'd asked. "I can certainly think about it, okay?"

"Don't worry about it. It was a crazy idea, *huh?*"

"No, I didn't think that. Hey, before I miss the turn"—he pointed toward a road sign directing him to a county road— "you said Shirt Lake, right?"

She nodded. "Yep, the turn is right up ahead."

Looking over at her now, her face full of strength, shining with a steadfast and serene peace, he knew he'd misjudged her when he'd found her in that ditch. She'd seemed so fragile. Now that he knew her a little more, she appeared to be an independent and courageous woman. She'd shaken off the accident rather quickly, where others might have panicked. And at first, she'd insisted that she was fine and didn't need to go to the hospital. But then she'd bucked up, and without concern for her car or a ride, she'd agreed. So far, she'd taken everything head-on and conquered it. Without a doubt, he knew she would have figured out a way to get to her home and back to her car.

Which reminded him. "I wanted to let you know, your car had some damage."

"And?" She looked over at him.

He smiled. "I had them take it to a friend's shop. He's already working on it as we speak."

"Really? What is wrong with it?"

"Well, a few minor problems from where you hit the deer. He's going to fix it enough to drive it. Then you can call your insurance and have them assess the damage and get the rest taken care of."

"Oh, okay, thanks."

"How long have you been coming up here?" He wanted to keep talking to her as well as lighten the somber mood she seemed to be in since he told her about her car.

"My parents lived up here until the mining industry collapsed. My dad needed a job, and Minneapolis seemed as good of a place as any to move to."

"How old were you?"

"Twelve."

"That sucks. I mean, the moving part. How is it, living in the Twin Cities?" Scott knew if something developed between them, he'd want to stay here. He couldn't ever see himself in a large city like Minneapolis.

"Oh, it has its ups and down. I came up here to get away from my hectic city life. I have this huge authors' conference next week that I've spent months putting together. That alone is overwhelming, but at the last minute, my star cover model canceled on me." She looked at her watch, and declared, "Right before I left on my trip, twelve hours or more ago. You know, I just realized, I've been up for over twenty-four hours. That's crazy, I haven't pulled an all-nighter since my college days."

Scott noticed the black circles surrounding her eyes. Reagan looked exhausted. He wanted to help her out and possibly get to know her more by spending more time with her.

"Okay, tell me a little more about what you need. As long as you agree to spend as much free time as you can spare getting to know me better, I'll do it. Even though I have no idea what I'm getting myself into."

She screamed, shattering the dead silence. "Oh my God! You've totally saved me. Thank you. I know it doesn't sound like a big deal, losing just one model. But, this guy was someone everyone expected. Still, as long as I replace him, most people won't mind. They just like the male models. You're going to be new to them, so it will be a great distraction to all my readers and authors. It's been a while since we had someone new."

"Well, I'm glad to be of service. You know, I wouldn't want to disappoint all those women."

"Some of these women can get pretty aggressive, if I lost someone and they came specifically for him. But, I'm hoping by explaining that he got sick and introducing you, it will be okay." She pushed her hair back away from her face.

"Do you really think they'd get angry for one model not coming? That seems insane to me?" Scott couldn't imagine all the pressure Reagan seemed to be putting on herself.

"Seriously, you don't know these women. They are vicious." She giggled, holding her side tightly. "Ouch, that really hurts."

He laughed with her, which only caused her to double over and giggle harder. She grabbed her side and bent over, moaning, "Oh shit."

Instantly, his good mood disappeared and in its place, concern and anxiety for her crept up. "Geez, you okay?"

She turned to look up at him, a smile brightening her face. Her thin jacket fell open, as did her button-up blouse, partially exposing her breast. His body careened into overdrive, and his libido kicked in. Shifting in the seat, he tried to readjust his position to relieve the stress against his zipper.

"I can't say anything about your readers and friends, but I have handled my share of women before being a cop. I have a suggestion, though."

"Anything you can suggest is welcomed in my crazy world."

* * *

Reagan couldn't believe her good fortune. Scott saved her from freezing to death. Well, not exactly, she wouldn't have died. But, he'd arranged for her car to be fixed enough to drive it back to the cities, and now, he was driving her to her parents' lake home.

Reagan wanted more than watching a beautiful sunrise, much more. Her stomach flip-flopped at the thought of spending the next week with him. Potentially, something she could only dream about or write in her stories.

How could Reagan, a romance author, explain to him that things like this didn't happen this fast in real life, especially when she couldn't explain it to herself?

"Would you like to come in, just for a minute?"

"Sure," They both got out of the car, meeting in the front of the vehicle. The driveway was a mess, the spring thaw and early morning warmth had already started to create mud, right in the path they needed to walk through to get up to the house.

"Dang it, look at this mess," she mumbled.

"No worries, let me help you." He grabbed her hand and helped her step around, and sometimes through, the soft ground.

Reagan tried hard not to step into the deeper mud and ruin her shoes. Not paying attention, she almost tripped, but Scott saved her again. He swung her up into his arms, and she squealed. "Oh, my…"

"I can't stand to see a damsel in distress," he teased.

She giggled, but grabbed onto him, putting her arms around his neck while he carried her the rest of the way up to the house.

Effortlessly, he walked up the steps. When he reached the front door, he let her slide down his body until her feet touched the cement. Sexual tension built inside of her while he patiently stood there, very close to her, waiting as she fished the keys out of her purse. He must have lost his patience, because she felt his hands before he spun her around and kissed her.

She felt her pulse leap with excitement. When he separated his body from hers, for a long moment, she felt as if she were floating.

"*Wow.*" Licking her lips, she enjoyed the taste of him. Peppermint and something else, maybe M&Ms? She wasn't sure but he was delicious. She touched his chest, but realized his uniform shirt was covered in mud.

He whispered into her hair, "Thank you."

"Come on in and take your shirt off, I'll get you one of my dad's."

She dashed to the back of the house to her parents' room. She grabbed a shirt then sprinted back into the living room. She stopped and dropped it.

There before her was the perfect body. Almost a Greek god. Perfection. His dark hair matched his complexion. She squatted and picked up the shirt before he noticed she'd joined him.

His brawny chest was flawless except for a thin white line below his pecs and across his ribs. Flinching slightly, she felt a chill cross her body. Realizing the pain he must have suffered upset her.

Tattoos covered his arms and shoulders. Not noticing that she had entered the room, he turned his back to her. A four-inch diagonal scar matching the one on his chest told her he'd been shot—entrance and exit wounds. Tats came around from the front, covering his shoulders and back.

Subconsciously, she licked her lips. He could be hers for the keeping. How she couldn't wait to get this man into her bed.

Smiling as if she was the cat that drank the milk, she cleared her throat. "*Um*... Scott?"

He spun around to face her. "*Huh?*"

"You know..." She slowly walked toward him, holding the shirt behind her back.

"Yes, 'you know' what?" He winked.

"*Um*..." She licked her lips again, slowly making her way to him.

"Do you like what you see?" he whispered, as he waited for her.

"Oh yeah," she murmured right before she reached him. She stood up on her tiptoes and kissed his lips, and at the same time, wrapped her arms around his neck.

"You sure about this, Reagan?" he whispered against her lips. He drew away from her slightly, brushing a kiss to the side of her neck. "Once I start, I won't stop."

"I don't want you to."

She knew she'd found the perfect man. This was just the beginning of an exciting new adventure, the time for her very own sweet romance. She decided to write under a new genre for this one.

The End

ABOUT THE AUTHOR

A little about me: I have two beautiful daughters, a son-in-law whom I adore, and an amazingly handsome grandson and a gorgeous granddaughter. I enjoy spending time with my family, love curling up with a good book, riding horses, saving every animal I can, and being with my German Shepherd, who is my constant companion and is unmercifully spoiled.

I was born and raised in Minnesota, and will continue my life here, though it does have its ups and down. This great state is known for its ten thousand lakes, along with green grass and big trees. Living here in this fine state, I find the seasons consist of road construction or winter, and it tends to wear on the soul. As I draw near retirement, I find myself wanting to leave this wonderful state and move somewhere warmer, but I will always find my way back home to Minnesota, as my children have made their lives here.

My friends and family will attest to the fact that I'm never far from a pen and paper. I find so many things in this world that pique my interest and inspire me to create an entire story.

If you'd like to contact me, you can reach me at lannafarrell.com or join me on Twitter @67lannafarrell or lanna.farrell.facebook.com.

TAKE YOUR SHIRT OFF & STAY FOREVER

THE BARN FIND
Ann Nardone

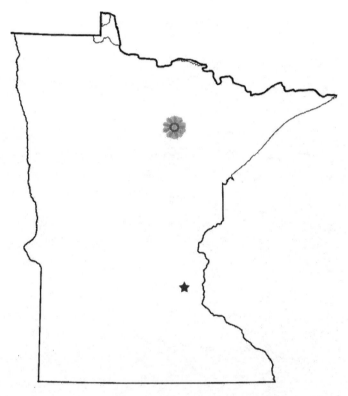

Bowstring Lake - Deer River, MN

"Sometimes a car can tell a story," the man said, as he wiped decades of dust off the old Chevy.

Lia didn't care if the car had a story. She just wanted to get rid of it—it and the old lady's lifetime of junk. Actually, she hadn't planned on putting the car on the market just yet. She had so many other things to deal with. Still, she happened to mention it to one of the employees at the store and the next morning, a guy called about it. Johnny La Forge was the son of the morning shift manager, and he was looking for a classic.

"Damn. A 1966 Impala. This is one bad-ass piece of mechanical engineering." He motioned to the hood. "Do you mind?"

She shrugged, which was all the consent he needed. He reached for some lever she couldn't see, and the hood popped open. "A big block, 396. And it's clean."

Lia couldn't imagine what was clean about anything in the barn. At least Johnny was nice to look at. He was about thirty, with thick dark hair and a lean, muscular build. Not that she was interested. Any guy who got so excited about an old car that didn't even run would not be her type.

"This is just amazing. How long has it been in here?" He didn't bother to look up from whatever had him so captivated.

"From what I understand, my great-aunt's son bought it new when he graduated from high school. He drove it for about a year, until he went to Vietnam. He parked it in here when he left and when he was killed in the war, she kept it, as a kind of memorial, I guess. She died last month."

Johnny straightened up and turned his head toward her. "I read about it in the paper. That's really sad."

"Yes, it is."

"I'm sorry. I didn't mean to..." He smiled sheepishly. "I just got a little carried away. This is quite a find."

"It's okay. We weren't close or anything. My dad was pretty much the only family she had left. Since he still has a career and I don't at the moment, he sent me up here to settle her affairs."

Why was she telling him this? At least she managed to stop herself before getting to the part about her boyfriend dumping her the same week she'd lost her job.

"That's too bad."

The sun was beaming through the wide doors, shining on him like a spotlight. Yes, he was very attractive. The last thing she wanted was Johnny feeling sorry for her.

"She was a nice lady. You'd have liked her, I think."

Lia frowned, confused for a second, and then realized he was talking about her great-aunt. "You knew her?"

That shouldn't have been surprising. His mother had probably managed Peterson's Store on Bow String for years. And anyway, in these little backwoods places, everyone knew everyone.

"Yeah, a little. Mrs. Peterson ran the store herself back when I was a kid. Sometimes she'd give us free candy or comic books. She was almost a legend around here. But I didn't know about her son."

Lia had always thought of Aunt Beverly as a recluse. Odd to hear such a different version of her from a stranger. Not that any of it mattered now. All that mattered was getting this mess cleaned up and squeezing as much cash out of it as possible. With enough work and luck, she could be finished and headed back to Minneapolis in a few weeks.

"Guess that's the story the car has to tell. A sad one."

Johnny shrugged. "Maybe I can give it something happier." He closed the hood. "Do you have the keys?"

"You don't think it'll run, do you?" She knew nothing about cars, but she had a feeling almost anything would be useless after sitting around for fifty years. Much as she wanted to sell the damn thing, she wasn't the type to take advantage of someone. If she were, she would have done better in the business world.

"Not now, no. I'd have to drain the old gasoline out and replace the battery. And it'll need new tires, of course, when the time comes. I just want to check out the interior."

As she handed the keys over to Johnny, Lia caught sight of his ring-less left hand. She reminded herself a guy like this was the last thing she needed. *What could they possibly have in common?* Not to mention she would be heading home in less than a month, with no reason to ever return. And he probably had a girlfriend, anyway.

She watched him unlock the driver's side door and slide behind the steering wheel. For some incomprehensible reason, he put the key into the ignition. Then he leaned over, reaching across the car's considerable width, and opened the passenger door.

"Wanna check it out?"

Lia had no interest in doing anything of the sort. But then, she figured sitting with a man she didn't know in a car that didn't run was a pretty good metaphor for her life at the moment. Being inside the old Chevy felt strange. Unlike the outside, the interior was mostly free of dust and grime. The vinyl seat felt new, the carpet looked clean—all of it untouched and unchanged for twice as many years as she'd been alive. She was starting to understand what the appeal might be.

"It's like a time machine."

"Exactly. You can almost feel the last people who were in here." He whistled a tune she recognized—The Beatles, *A Day in the Life*.

"What was his name? Mrs. Peterson's son?" Johnny asked after they sat a few minutes soaking up the old energy the Impala still held.

"Kenneth." Lia recalled hearing her father mention him a few times over the years, but until now, she'd never thought much about him.

Johnny ran his hand over the beautifully preserved dash pad, as though petting a kitten. "He must have saved up a long time to buy this car. Working at the family store, probably. Think how proud of it he must have been. A young kid like that. A powerful car. I'll bet he felt like one big deal cruising around in this."

"But only for a year."

She eyed the dashboard, noting the radio but not recognizing the numbers of the AM stations. She wondered if, with a new battery, it would still play music. Then her eyes fell to the glove box. It opened easily, but the light in the barn was too dim to make out its contents.

"Do you have—" she started to ask when he held up his cell phone and faced it into the small space.

Lia pulled out the contents. A Minnesota highway map, a pair of plastic sunglasses, and a small wooden box with *Peterson's Store on Bowstring Lake* burned into the cover.

"I remember these," Johnny said. "The store was still selling them to the tourists when I was a kid."

"Why would he have carried this around?"

"I don't know. See what's in it."

Her hand rested on the smooth, polished wood. "It feels kind of intrusive."

"Pretty sure he's not going to mind."

"Well, yeah." She tried to shoot him a dirty look but was caught off-guard by the excitement showing in his eyes. Sitting so close to him, she could see they were brown, with flecks of honey.

The car was telling its story. She lifted the lid.

"I want a better look at this," she said. It was true, but there was more to it.

He scooted over toward her, which made her pleasantly uncomfortable. She did not need this. Clutching the box, Lia hurried out of the Chevy and the barn.

From the front yard of Aunt Beverly's house, she could see downhill to the store and beyond it to the sparkling water of Bowstring Lake. With fishing season just underway, both appeared busy. The surreal sense of timelessness she'd felt inside the Impala vanished. Johnny came up behind her. She could feel him looking over her shoulder.

Nestled in the box were two high school rings, one large and heavy, the other small and delicate. The boy's ring was from Deer River High School, class of 1966 with the initials *KWP* engraved on the inside. Not surprising. Lia had expected it to belong to Kenneth. She clasped it in her hand, trying again to get a feel for this young boy her aunt had spent the rest of her life mourning. Then she placed it gently back into the container that had held it for so long and turned her attention to its companion.

The girl's ring was also from Deer River High, but this time the class of '67. She read the initials aloud. "*J-A-L*. Does that mean anything to you?"

"No, but that's not much to go on." He took the ring from her and turned it between his fingers. "My mom might know. She was younger, but maybe Mrs. Peterson said something to her."

He handed the ring back to Lia. She returned it to the box and removed the last remaining item, a folded piece of notebook paper.

"I'm not sure I should read this," she said, as she opened it to reveal a few rows of feminine handwriting. "I know he's dead but she's probably still alive."

Johnny stepped back and crossed his arms over his chest. "I understand you don't feel right about it but, c'mon, aren't you curious?"

"Yeah"—she smiled a little—"I am. Besides, it's not like she'll know, right?"

She handed the box to Johnny so she could clutch the letter in both hands. In a soft, steady voice she read. "'Dear Kenny, I may not be here when you get back, but I promise you will always be in my heart and I will love you forever. I just know that somehow, some way, we will be together again.' It's signed Janet."

"*Huh*." Johnny rubbed his chin, absentmindedly. "Wonder what that means."

"It is kind of weird." She refolded the letter and put it back next to the rings, where it had laid for so long.

"I don't really want to put this back in the car. Maybe I'll bring it into the house."

"*Umm*...speaking of the car, what's your asking price?"

She had almost forgotten what brought Johnny to see her in the first place. Not being a car person at all, she had no idea how much it was worth. "Would you like to make an offer?"

He smiled. "You know, I could really take advantage of you right now. But I won't. Do some research and decide what you want for it. Then we'll talk."

Wow, she really was a terrible businesswoman. No wonder she was unemployed. "Sure. I'll get back to you tomorrow."

"See you then. And, Lia?" He took a step closer so he was looking into her eyes. She suddenly wished she'd put on makeup and done something with her hair. "This whole little historic investigation...it was fun. Let's see it through."

She nodded. "I plan to."

Lia watched as he walked down the driveway, climbed into his Ford pickup, and drove away. She felt a little sorry to see him leave.

* * *

Lia had settled into the upstairs bedroom previously occupied by Aunt Beverly's caregiver. The bed was comfortable enough and she was extremely tired but sleep would not come. It was too dark, too quiet, and she had too much on her mind. Worries regarding money, finding a new job, and selling the damn store still haunted her, but tonight her thoughts kept returning to Kenneth and JAL, to the car, and to Johnny La Forge. 'See the investigation through,' he'd said. She didn't have time for that. *So why was she so intent on solving it? A distraction from all her troubles, maybe?*

She got up and wrapped her old terry cloth robe around her body. The floor was cold against her bare feet. It had been warm during the day, but once the sun set, a chill moved in. She intended to go down to the kitchen and make a cup of tea, but found herself instead staring at the room across the hall. The room once belonging to Kenneth.

Unlike the car, her great-aunt Beverly hadn't kept the room as a shrine. Instead, it had become a sort of junk room. Lia glanced through some of it when she'd first arrived and made plans to do a more detailed survey when she got a chance. But she remembered many of Kenneth's things were stored in there—including his high school yearbooks.

Deer River High was a small school so it didn't take too long to find what she was looking for. There was only one girl in the class of '67 who fit the first name and initials on the ring. Janet Alice Lawery was a fair-haired girl, with a heart-shaped face and a pretty smile. In the small black and white photo, she looked happy.

Thoughts of the note left in the Impala flooded her mind. There were far more important things to worry about, and yet she found herself desperately wanting to know more about Janet and Kenneth. The old car left to rot in the barn was calling to her. Not in the way it called to Johnny.

He felt the need to restore it.

She needed to understand its secrets.

* * *

Johnny went to the Peterson place as soon as he got off work. He'd called ahead, so Lia was waiting for him, standing outside in the yard. Her dark red hair was down today, and she was wearing a V-neck shirt. It shouted out what an attractive woman she was far better than the over-sized sweatshirt she'd worn yesterday. He waved and climbed out of the truck as she smiled and waved back. He hadn't noticed earlier what a beautiful smile she had.

The business he'd come to discuss didn't take long. They sat together at Mrs. Peterson's kitchen table while Johnny made a formal offer. It was clear she still didn't have a clue how much the car was worth. He could have easily cheated her, but he didn't. He liked to think he wouldn't cheat anybody.

And he had to admit he kind of liked her. She seemed a bit less grumpy than before. Maybe he'd misjudged her.

"I can have it towed," Johnny said, once the papers were signed and the money had changed hands. "But if it's all right with you, I'd like to get to work on it here. I'm hoping to drive it home."

Lia's face widened with surprise and maybe a hint of amusement. "You really think you can get that old thing to run? I mean, like, without rebuilding it or whatever?"

"I sure do. Got all I need in the back of my truck."

She shrugged. "Be my guest."

He started to push his chair back, eager to get to work.

"*Umm*..." Lia reached across the table, almost but not quite, touching his hand. "You remember the note we found in the car?"

Of course he did. It added another layer to his amazing find. "Sure."

She grinned. He wondered again how he hadn't seen before how hot she was. "I found something."

As anxious as Johnny was to get the car running, he found himself growing interested as Lia showed him the old yearbook. Lia leaned in close to him as they looked at the picture.

"Do you know her?" Lia asked. "Or her kids?"

He shook his head. "Never heard of her. I could ask my parents but...a lot of people don't stick around here after they graduate. From the note, it sounds like she was leaving. I'm guessing she moved away a long time ago."

"I know." She sighed, a very sexy sigh. "Was just kind of hoping. I would love to find her. Maybe give her the ring back. I suppose that sounds silly."

"No, it doesn't." He resisted the urge to slip his arm around her shoulder. "I think it's kind of sweet."

"Well, then I think I'll try to Google her. She probably got married and changed her name, but it's worth a shot."

"Even if we can't meet with her in person, you can leave her a message. She might think it's cool to get a little blast from the past." He stood up. "I'm going to get started on the Chevy. Let me know if you find anything."

He paused at the door for a few seconds then went out to the barn.

* * *

Lia carried her iPad out to the porch. The day was too perfect to be indoors. The warm breeze smelled of lilac, pine, and fresh grass. Down the hill, Bowstring Lake was dotted with fishing boats. The number would probably double come the weekend, bringing needed business to the store. Until she could rid herself of the Peterson property, she might as well make the best of it.

Reluctantly, she tore her eyes from the view and typed, *Janet Alice Lawery, Deer River, Minnesota,* into the search engine. She expected a lot of useless partial matches and advertisements. What she found instead sent a chill down her spine.

According to an article from the *Duluth Tribune* dated June 21, 1967, Janet Lawery was reported missing by her parents. She was last seen walking down an old logging road just north of Bowstring Lake.

She wasn't sure how many hours she spent combing the internet for something else regarding Janet's disappearance. She only knew that she'd found nothing. Whatever ending she'd had in mind when she'd started her little investigation, this was definitely not it.

When she first went into the barn, she thought Johnny somehow left without her noticing. Then she noticed a pair of boots sticking out from under the car.

"Johnny?" Lia waited until he crawled out and stood up. His hands and clothes were covered in grease, and there was a large smear on the side of his cheek. "Look at this."

He wiped his palms on the front of his jeans before he took the iPad from her. She watched a frown spread over his face as he read.

"So what happened?" He handed it back to her.

"No idea. That's all I could find. But I was thinking, there can't be a whole lot of people who go missing in a place like this. So, if it happens, wouldn't people talk about it for years? I mean, wouldn't you have heard of it?"

"I never have and I'd remember." He pushed a strand of hair off his forehead. "Sometimes small towns don't talk about things they'd rather forget."

"Yeah, I guess you're right. How are we going to find out what happened to her?"

"Lia," he said, then stopped as though trying to choose the right words. "If she's been missing all this time, there probably isn't a way to find her."

"I know. I know. I never should have gotten so caught up in this." She gave a small, humorless laugh. "It's not like the answer is going to be right in front of us."

Johnny looked over his shoulder at the Impala. "Unless, maybe it is."

"What do you mean?" The icky feeling stirring in her stomach told her she already knew.

She followed as he walked slowly around to the back of the car. They stood together, staring down at it.

"You don't think..."

"God, I hope not. But it kind of makes sense."

"Wouldn't there be a...a smell or something?"

"Well, yeah, initially. But after all this time, I don't think there would, you know, be enough left."

"So, we need to look."

He nodded and dug the keys out of his pocket. Lia held her breath and fought the urge to close her eyes, as Johnny popped the trunk.

The old Chevy's big trunk held a spare tire, a tire iron, and a bag of road salt. Nothing more. They sighed in unison. After another second, he started to laugh and she joined him. They laughed together until her side hurt and she had to suck in a sharp breath.

"Looks like we got a little carried away," he said, once he had himself under control.

Lia wiped a tear from the corner of eye. "Think so?"

"Hey, it wasn't such a crazy idea. I mean, if she is dead, gotta wonder where he dumped her."

"Are you talking about Kenneth?"

"Well, he had to get rid of her somewhere. And he was leaving the car shut up in here. Then again, I imagine the cops would have searched this property."

"You sound pretty convinced he killed her."

"Come on. If anyone killed her, it was probably him."

"How can you say that?" She felt a hot tide of anger rising up in her chest. "You never even knew him."

"Neither did you." Lia started to answer but Johnny held up his hand to stop her. "I'm just saying, statistically when a woman is murdered it's usually her husband or boyfriend."

"Yeah?" She folded her arms across her chest and glared at him. "How many girlfriends did you kill?"

"What? Hey, don't get all pissed off. I'm just saying—"

"Statistically. I know." She turned on her heel and stormed out.

She could hear Johnny calling after her, but she ignored him. Without so much as a backward glance, she went into the house and straight up the stairs. It didn't take her long to find what she was looking for. She remembered where she'd seen it during her search of Kenneth's room the night before. She paused only long enough to check out what it actually said, then marched back to the barn.

He was still standing there, staring at the door as though he was debating whether or not to follow her. Well, fine. She'd saved him the trouble.

"Here." She held up the papers from Kenneth's time in the Army. "You can see in June of 1967, Kenneth had already been deployed. So, unless he somehow teleported back here from Vietnam, he did not kill Janet."

"Yeah, good," he said. "Great. It's not that I wanted him to be the killer."

"Well, now you know he wasn't."

She intended to stomp off again, but clearing Kenneth's name in Johnny's eyes cooled her anger.

"I'm sorry," he said at last. "Look, I get that he was family. And he was Mrs. Peterson's son. I should've had more respect."

Lia nodded, then realized she was probably coming off as more smug than she intended.

"He was. And even though I never knew him, in fact, I didn't even know my great-aunt Beverly that well, I kind of feel like I did. You know?"

"I can see that." She must have looked skeptical. "I really can. Working on this car, his car, I'm kind of feeling the same way." He sounded sincere. "It's almost like I'm getting the car going for him. I mean, yeah, of course I'm doing it for me. But it seems like it's a memorial to him."

"And a way to make up for accusing him of murder?"

He grinned a little sheepishly. "Yes, that too."

She needed to go back into the house, to box up items for donations, to price things for the estate sale, to let Johnny get back to work. *What was she waiting for?*

"Maybe that's how I feel about finding Janet. Or finding out what happened to her. It would be a sort of memorial."

"Then do it," Johnny said. "You can ask questions around town, maybe find a retired cop or reporter who can tell you something. Who knows, maybe you can still find another clue in the house. Or the car."

At least he didn't think she was crazy. He understood. She wished she could tell him how much that meant to her. "I think I will keep looking. There wasn't anything else left in the car, though, was there?" She opened the Chevy's passenger side door and looked into the glove box. "Just a road map."

Johnny shrugged. "You must have a lot of stuff in the house."

"Way too much."

With a parting smile to let him know she was no longer angry, far from it in fact, she went back to the house.

On a hunch, she spread the old map out on the table. The state of Minnesota as it had been in the 60's stretched out in front of her. Whatever she wanted to find, it wasn't there. She flipped it over.

The backside was specifically Itasca County. She was about to fold it back up when she noticed a flash of red ink. She squinted, trying to see if it was a circle or a heart. Either way, it was on a wooded spot north of Bowstring Lake.

Lia shouldn't have been this excited. It might possibly lead to something. But, she was also aware it could be nothing but a fool's errand.

She could waste time running around town asking everyone over sixty what they remembered about Janet instead of getting the store sold. She could search through every memento her great-aunt Beverly ever kept instead of getting the junk out of here. After all that, she might find an answer. Or she might not.

And what would it matter to her anyway? Sure, Johnny thought she should pursue it, but he also thought he could get a car back on the road after almost fifty years in a barn.

Then, just as she was about to put the map away and get back to her real work, she heard something from inside the barn. The sound of an engine roaring back to life.

* * *

They next day, they took the Impala out for a drive. Lia leaned back against the seat, the vinyl hot from the sunlight. Johnny looked as happy and proud as a new father behind the wheel. She wished some of his mood would rub off on her and calm the icy fingers gripping her stomach. Lia could not decide if she was more worried they wouldn't find anything or that they would.

They'd spent the previous evening looking over the map and deciding what the next step would be. After buying a pizza at the store, they ate it on her front porch until the rain shower blew in and drove them into the house. He told her about his life, about his job with the Fish and Wildlife Service at Cut Foot Sioux. They stayed at the kitchen table talking until long after the sky cleared and turned dark. When he leaned in to hug her goodbye, she got the feeling he wanted to kiss her. She thought she might want him to.

He left in his pickup late at night, promising to be back in the morning.

Johnny had warned that if the seldom-used road was too rough, they would have to park the car and walk. "You need to be careful with a classic," he said, patting the dashboard.

"So, we're looking for a dirt road?"

He shrugged. "Maybe. It might not be much more than a path."

"Do you think it'll be a cabin or something?"

"Might just be a hunting shack. Could be nothing in that spot at all, either because there never was or because whatever had been there is gone now."

Lia's stomach flipped again as the darkest possibilities flashed through her mind.

Johnny slowed the Chevy to a halt. "Is this it?"

She traced her finger along the map. "According to this, it is."

She looked up. Instead of the rustic trail they'd expected, there was an actual road, narrow and nearly hidden, but tarred.

"There's been new building going on over the years," Johnny said. "I just didn't think there was much this far from the lake."

Disappointment replaced fear in her mind. "I guess we should check it out anyway."

Three miles down the road they came to a house. Although located in about the spot marked on Kenneth's map, it couldn't be what they were searching for. The small, tidy cottage couldn't have been more than ten years old, by Lia's estimation.

They sat at the end of driveway, staring.

"What do we do now?" she asked. "Start asking around town?"

"We've come this far"—Johnny pulled the key out of the ignition—"might as well check it out."

"We can't just go knock on the door."

Johnny laughed. "You're not in the city now. People are friendlier up here."

Standing on the steps, Lia scrambled for what to say if anyone answered their knock. She hoped Johnny had something in mind. But when the door opened and she looked into the face of the woman who answered, she knew what to say. Her hair was gray, and there were lines around her eyes and mouth, but she was still pretty.

"Janet Lawery?" Lia blurted out before Johnny could finish

saying, "Hello."

"That was my maiden name." Her expression was questioning but not unfriendly.

"I'm Lia, Kenneth Peterson was my dad's cousin. I wanted to meet you."

"Kenny? I haven't heard that name in long time." Her smile was wistful. "You know, my family owned this land for generations. Kenny and I were going to build our house on it. I thought of him when I decided to retire here."

"So, you were away a long time?" Johnny sounded hesitant.

Lia knew what he was trying to ask and she saw his point in not being direct. "We were looking into Kenneth's life and found a newspaper article that said you'd disappeared."

"Disappeared?" She shook her head. "I suppose I did. I ran away. Oh, it was a stupid, reckless thing to do, but I was eighteen. Angry Kenny had gone off to war, mad at my parents for 'not getting it,' tired of living in the sticks. So, I hitchhiked to California."

"Wow," Johnny said, sounding impressed. "To be a hippie?"

"Not exactly, but something like that. Those were the times."

"You just dropped everything and took off? That's pretty cool," Lia said.

"I did have some adventures. Then I realized I was being stupid and came home. I thought I'd be waiting for Kenny." Her voice quivered on his name.

"Then what did you do?"

"Went off to college. Got a job down south. Met a man. Had children and grandchildren. Funny, though, I ended up right back here."

Her eyes looked past them, down the drive, and she let out a gasp. "Is that...?"

"Kenneth's car," Johnny said. "I just got it going."

"Oh my God." She brushed past them and walked down the driveway. "It looks the same."

She circled around it, her eyes glistening. "He loved this car. He would be happy to see it like this. Still young, still beautiful, after all these years."

"I think he'd be happy to see how good you look after all these years." Johnny flashed a charming smile.

"Well, aren't you sweet." Janet laughed through her tears. "Thank you. I mean, thank you for letting me see his car again."

"Thank you," said Lia. "You gave us the answers to some questions we had." Another thought popped into her head. "Would you like your class rings back? Yours and his? I can bring them to you."

"And when you do, maybe you can take me for a ride?"

"With pleasure."

They said their goodbyes and Janet turned back to her house.

"Have a good Memorial Day," Johnny called.

She looked back at them. "I just did."

* * *

They drove back to the Peterson place, but instead of going to the house, they parked next to the lake.

"It's beautiful here." Without thinking, Lia rested her head against Johnny's shoulder.

"I thought you couldn't wait to get back to the Cities." He put his arm around her.

"I thought so too, at first. But now..." She looked up at him. "I don't really have anything to go back to. I'm thinking maybe I'll stay. Live in Beverly's house and run the store."

He smiled. "Looks like I found my dream car and my dream girl all in the same day."

She leaned in to meet his kiss. "See, you never know what you're going to find in a barn."

ABOUT THE AUTHOR

Ann Nardone's stories appear in Romancing the Lakes Summer, Fall, and Winter anthologies. She balances writing with working at her job, raising her teenagers, caring for a menagerie of pets and spending time with her husband and his beloved '66 Impala. She lives in Farmington.

ABOUT THE MINNESOTA LAKES WRITERS

Living in Minnesota, surrounded by lakes, *Minnesota Lakes Writers* can't help creating stories of being up North at the cabin, in town at one of the city lakes or Minnesota's own massive Lake Superior. No matter what time of year it is, there is always something going on at the lake. Hey, it's Minnesota! Whether you are sitting on a dock listening to loons calling, taking a leisurely walk around a lake, cruising the lake on a boat or just sitting on a beach, for writers, ideas form and stories begin.

These writers enjoy getting together to set in motion scary stories to be told under the evening stars at a beach campfire or on the frozen ice of Minnesota's winter lakes. And, of course, romances set on sandy lakeshores or on boats skimming over gentle waves.

Minnesota Lakes Writers write stories about Minnesota and its lakes encompassing romance, mystery, and fantasy. Our goal is to enjoy each other's love of writing and tell stories about Minnesota and its 10,000 lakes. And since there are so many, it may take us a while!

For more information, find us on our website at www.minnesotalakeswriters.blogspot.com.

ALSO AVAILABLE BY OUR AUTHORS

ANGELINE FORTIN

Time Travel Romance Novels:
A Laird for All Time
Nothing But Time
My Heart's in the Highlands
A Time and Place for Every Laird
Taken
Love in the Time of a Highland Laird

Questions for a Highlander *Historical Romance Novel Series:*
A Question of Love
A Question of Lust
A Question of Trust
The Perfect Question
A Question for Harry
A Question Worth Asking (Coming Summer 2016)

Short Stories:
The Leap in *Romancing the Lakes of Minnesota—Autumn*
Alone with the Devil in *Romancing the Lakes of Minnesota—Winter*
In the Holiday Spirit in *Spirits of the Season*

PEG PIERSON

Paranormal Romance Novels:
Flirting with Fangs

Short Stories:
Fish Flirt Too in *Romancing the Lakes of Minnesota—Autumn*
A Southern Spark on Northern Ice in *Romancing the Lakes of Minnesota—Winter*

DYLANN CRUSH

Short Stories:
Love Under the Northern Lights in *Romancing the Lakes of Minnesota—Winter*

KRISTY JOHNSON

Short Stories:
Light Bender in *Romancing the Lakes of Minnesota—Summer*
Cara's Swim in *Romancing the Lakes of Minnesota—Autumn*
Frozen on Lake Superior in *Romancing the Lakes of Minnesota—Winter*

KATIE CURTIS

Short Stories:
Lady Sylvia's Spell in *Romancing the Lakes of Minnesota—Summer*
Third Time's a Charm in *Romancing the Lakes of Minnesota—Autumn*
Wish Upon the North Star in *Romancing the Lakes of Minnesota—Winter*

ROSE MARIE MEUWISSEN

Contemporary Romance Novel:
Taking Chances

Short Stories:
Dancing in the Moonlight in *Love in the Land of Lakes Anthology*
Hot Summer Nights in *Romancing the Lakes of Minnesota—Summer*
Railroad Ties in *Romancing the Lakes of Minnesota—Autumn*

Blizzard of Love in *Romancing the Lakes of Minnesota—Winter*

Children's Books:
Real Norwegians Eat Lutefisk
Real Norwegians Eat Rommegrot

INGRID ANDERSON SAMPO

Short Stories:
Loon Racing in *Romancing the Lakes of Minnesota—Summer*
Cup a' Java in *Romancing the Lakes of Minnesota—Autumn*
Power to the Sixties in *Romancing the Lakes of Minnesota—Winter*

DIANE WIGGERT

Short Stories:
Magic at Moose Lake in *Romancing the Lakes of Minnesota—Autumn*
Love's No Joke in *Romancing the Lakes of Minnesota—Winter*

LANNA FARRELL

Contemporary Romance Novels:
Steel Toes to Stilettos Series
Short Fuse to Happiness – Book One
Eighteen Wheels to Heaven – Book Two

Holiday Cheer Series
The Spook & the Hacker – Book One
A Grateful Heart – Book Two
A Christmas Stalking – Book Three

Beneath the Lies – Book Four
Out of the Darkness – Book Five

Livingston Agency Series
You Belong to Me – Book One

The Remington Series
Matheau – Book One
Lillianna – Book Two

Dark Tribal Brotherhood Series
Brazen Rose – Book One

ANN NARDONE

Short Stories:
Putting Demons to Rest in *Romancing the Lakes of Minnesota*—Summer
For the Love of Bertha in *Romancing the Lakes of Minnesota*—Autumn
Before the Trail Goes Cold in *Romancing the Lakes of Minnesota*—Winter

Made in the USA
Charleston, SC
02 May 2016